The Failure Cascade

Also by Jon Konrath

Fiction:

Ranch: The Musical (2019)

Book of Dreams (2018)

Help Me Find My Car Keys and We Can Drive Out! (2017)

Vol. 13 (2016)

He (2015)

The Memory Hunter (2014)

Atmospheres (2014)

Thunderbird (2013)

Sleep Has No Master (2012)

The Earworm Inception (2012)

Fistful of Pizza (2011)

Rumored to Exist (2002)

Summer Rain (2000)

Nonfiction:

The Necrokonicon (2006)

Dealer Wins (2004)

Tell Me a Story About the Devil (2003)

The Failure Cascade

Jon Konrath

¶|

Paragraph Line Books
Oakland, CA
http://www.paragraphline.com

For more information, please visit
http://www.rumored.com

ISBN: 978-1-942086-17-8

PL-129 (v2)

The Semiotics of Stupidity

I keep having a recurring nightmare that I'm a professional wrestler and I'm fighting someone in a Sbarro pizza at the mall. He's beating me to death with a parmesan cheese shaker wrapped in barbed wire and yelling a catchphrase, something about canned ham. I've got blood all over my forehead, and cheese dust in my eyes. Mick Foley also works at the pizza place, but he called in sick that day.

The Czechoslovakian Monster Energy Drink Conundrum

Peter Tork's mother invented napalm. Or maybe it was Krazy Glue. I tried looking this up online, but it was the week he died, and every result I could possibly find was an "article" that was a tweet that was a share of a video that was a TV story of some random person like Harlan Ellison or the BTK Killer or Alexander Haig giving the Monkees musician a shout-out. Tork's wiki page had ten thousand edits per second for twenty-four hours straight after his death was announced. Most of them were links to amateur snuff films, herbal diabetes remedies, and used coffin dealers in Louisiana. There was a trend there, but I don't know what. Cheer up, sleepy Jean.

Fell down a family tree k-hole during my search, started reading about viral marketing, soft drink promotions, and taurine. There was a thing going on that week where anyone who could prove they were born in Czechoslovakia got a free can of Monster Energy Drink. There were some other limitations — identity theft is rampant in the former communist country; 80% of their passports and ID cards are forgeries — but they gave away millions of dollars of product, mostly to old pensioners who wanted to cure Parkinson's disease with massive doses of caffeine. I was 14% sure I had a great-great-great-uncle from Prague who hated condoms. If I could find an old census, maybe I could score some free beverages.

"Those things are bullshit," Fast Eddie said. We were in the 7-Eleven looking at slutty biker magazines and trying to get something to keep us awake for the next week. (I know I've written about thirteen other stories about me and an old buddy hanging out at 7-Eleven looking at slutty biker magazines. There's not a lot to do in Indiana, give me a break.) "Five bucks for a can of carbonated Kool-Aid with a little bit of a buzz. Total waste of money. I did get hooked on 5-Hour Energy for a while, because I heard on the news it was killing people, and why the fuck would you want to be alive in this town? Didn't do shit for me, though."

"You should try Rip It," I said. "I hear that stuff's primo. Everyone in my alien abduction support group drinks like a case a day. Totally safe. I mean, four of them have died from an aortic dissection, but I don't think it's related."

"Isn't that the one everyone in the Army abuses?"

"Yeah, totally. They feed it to Apache helicopter pilots so they can shoot civilians faster. And it's the same maker as Faygo, so you've got the Insane Clown Posse thing going."

"Fuck ICP," he said. "And fuck KISS, too. Only King Diamond should wear black and white face makeup. And maybe black metal bands, but only if they've burned down a church. Do they still make Jolt Cola? At least that stuff had extra sugar and didn't taste like you were blowing Willy Wonka with the stupid artificial fruit flavoring."

I hadn't thought about Jolt in years, and wondered if it was still available. I remember one summer in the late eighties, being stuck in Rochester, New York — or maybe it was Buffalo. I was trying to take pictures of evergreen trees for some stupid high school multimedia project, but my Vivitar point-and-shoot film camera got stuck and I snapped twenty-four images on top of each other, so it looked like a nightmarish modern art disaster when I got the film developed. And this was years before Instagram, where I could have told people it was an obscure Sonic Youth European B-side cover and gotten a million likes. Totally wasted trip, except that I found a Wegman's that sold Jolt in cans and glass bottles, and I sucked down a six-pack a night and couldn't shit or sleep for a week. It was glorious.

I have this Mandela thing where I think that Combos snacks were also invented around the same time, but they actually came out in the mid-seventies, and this must have been more an issue with growing up in a small town where people thought Heinz ketchup was too spicy, and they first discovered the Macarena around 2007. I used to love Combos. Perfect road trip snack. I can eat an unlimited amount of the cheddar cheese variety without getting sick of them, like a bag a day for a year straight. Cheddar cheese pretzel Combos are the absolute best. The cheddar cheese crackers are okay, but they're kind of bullshit because they aren't encrusted in salt that will someday kill me. The pizza ones are decent, but aside from the lack of a pretzel configuration with the blessed extra salt, they have the synthetic taste of fake pizza like the chemical they put in scratch-and-sniff pizza stickers, or school lunch pizza, which makes me retch. I know people say they love school lunch pizza, especially the hexagon-shaped Mexican pizza. These people are wrong, and most likely have a dodgeball-related traumatic head injury. Plus about 167% of the people who say they like Mexican pizza from school lunch hate Mexicans, so maybe they should sort that out first and shut the fuck up.

While I was deep in my flavor daydream, Fast Eddie got in a fight with a school librarian dressed as a cop loitering by the nacho cheese and chili machines. She had a fake badge, a fake uniform, and a plastic BB gun that looked like an Uzi, with the orange barrel spray-painted black. I think she gave him shit for reading pornography in a public place because he spent a little too long looking at a Lita Ford layout in a *Metal Edge* magazine. They traded sissy punches until Eddie jammed his thumb from having it inside his fist, and I had to listen to him bitch about how he almost could have won the fight while I brought him to the hospital so he could try to score Vicodin.

¯_(ツ)_/¯

Everything in this book is 100% true, including this statement.

* * *

My stepdad broke both of his arms in a drunken feats-of-strength contest when my older brother was two, and he spent the better part of his childhood thinking it was normal that a wife had to wipe her husband's ass every time he took a dump. (My brother thought this, not my stepdad. Well, maybe my stepdad too. But I wasn't born yet. I should probably plug some names in that sentence so it makes more sense, but I don't want to imply anything, because this is a work of fiction.)

* * *

I went to Target the other day and the new Mariah Carey autobiography was in the fiction section.

On a Wavelength Far From Home

...Atomic submarines, launching Trident II missiles from the shores of Lake Erie, something about a first-strike nuclear attack against the Cleveland Cavaliers to lower their salary cap. I wear SPF-50 sun cream, nothing to worry about here. Put in a pair of foam earplugs I stole from work, the bright orange kind, just in case the explosions got a bit too spicy. My stereo was loud enough to drown out most of it (Alpine head unit; Alpine four-channel amp; Pioneer 6x9 speakers in back, 6-inch 3-ways in the doors, gold-plated, oxygen-free cables all around), but better safe than sorry.

"Got me a bad case of laminitis. Hurts every time the moon is full." A Unabomber-looking man clad in a Camel Cash windbreaker in front of the Speedway station tried hustling me for lottery ticket money. Woe is me, I have a crippling inflammation, I need five bucks to get a Joker's Wild scratcher. I knew he was full of shit — only hoofed animals, horses and cows, can get laminitis. Maybe goats, I didn't bother looking it up. I let the guy ramble while I pumped half a paycheck into the 22-gallon tank in my land yacht. It took twenty minutes to fill the damn thing, and the car only got ten miles to a gallon, so I spent a lot of my day listening to crazy people offer to wash my windows or beg for money.

Best way to lose this guy so I can buy a bunch of junk food? "Hey buddy, the Space Shuttle's exploding!" Point at the nuclear explosions on the horizon, make a run for the mini-mart. I bought a 55-gallon garbage bag of off-brand kettle chips encrusted in some sort of fake mesquite barbecue dust that looked like dirt from the surface of Mars, and a six-liter bottle of ice-cold RC Cola. Jumped back in the car through the window Bo and Luke Duke style and hit the road.

...Guy on the radio said ghosts walk through walls because buildings get remodeled, and the doors and windows are moved to different places. Blame it all on HGTV, sure. I cannot take ghost hunters seriously, because every one I meet is conceal-carrying six guns and has removed the catalytic converter from his car in a "fuck libtards" rage. Seriously, how is shooting a home intruder going to work if their soul haunts you for all of eternity? Either get a trap and a containment unit from *Ghostbusters*, or shut the fuck up.

There's a channel on XM that's in the 9000s, way the hell up there on the dial (not that radios have dials anymore) that plays nothing but Boston songs backwards, so you can appreciate how much Tom Scholz used back-masking to prove his allegiance to Satan. Or maybe it was just signal noise from those Rockman pre-amps he hand-built back in the day. I'm not a recording engineer, just a guy with too much time on his hands who has a perpetual XM subscription because I call every thirty days and threaten to quit, so I get another month free. (No wonder their stock is always in the shitter.)

I listen to inverse-Boston and take Ambien by the dozen so I can drive while I'm asleep. Seems counter-intuitive, but I can do anything better asleep than awake, apparently. One time I completely rebuilt a 1974 AMC Matador as a rally racing car, with a full roll cage and a beefed-up 6.6-liter engine built from AMC's service replacement heavy-duty block with four-bolt mains, like Penske Racing used on their AMC Javelin T/A racing vehicles. That was before Ambien was invented. I think I abused Seconal back then, can't remember.

* * *

"You'd think AMC cars would be on the AMC TV station the most, but they're not." I sat shotgun in the cop car and tried to make small talk while he wrote me a ticket for driving while asleep. (Actually the state didn't have an ordinance about driving while asleep, so he had to give me a speeding ticket. This was a state where it was still legal to drink and drive, so sleeping was definitely not an issue.) There wasn't a shotgun in the front of the car, which would be awesome, because I could steal it. Instead of the standard-issue Mossberg 12-gauge, the cop had a corn dog in the dash-mounted rifle holder. At least the car was air conditioned;

my giant boat of a car allegedly had AC, but it barely put out lukewarm air, and only when you got above 100 MPH, which was almost never. "The AMC channel had a lot of old Chevy cars on there, mostly cop cars. And *Mad Men* had that whole GM plot. Christ, do you remember that redhead's tits? Each one was bigger than a prize-winning watermelon at the 4-H county fair..."

The cop ignored me, scribbled down my info on the ticket, and waited for the check to see if I had any outstanding warrants. Most podunk cities in the center of the state made all their revenue writing bullshit tickets on the highway. Instead of schools and fire and hospitals, their entire budget went to Ford Police Interceptors and radar guns. And the trick is, you could go to court and fight a ticket, but if you're an out-of-towner, it was easier to pay the fine immediately than take a day off work and drive six hours into the middle of nowhere and sit around a village too small to even have a Subway restaurant hanging off the side of a gas station. Hell, they knew this would happen so much, the cop cars had Visa machines built into the dashboard. I think they even took American Express and Discover. Decided to roll the bones and not pay for it, try my luck with the judge. Besides, my 500$-limit Visa had about 497$ of junk on it.

He wrote "thank the lord!" and put a smiley face on the back of the ticket, like a dumpy waitress trying to get a tip would write on the back of a check in a truck stop diner. He then wasted another ten minutes of my time telling a story about how some kids in the next town bought a pound of black tar heroin off the internet, and he got to impound their vehicles and burn their houses down, no judge or jury. "Those drug laws are the best darn thing to happen to small-town police since the glory hole was invented. We don't get cable TV out here. A house-burning is almost as good as that UFC fighting stuff they have in the city."

* * *

...Out again, woke up in the back seat of the car in the parking lot of a Mr. Wiggs department store, sucking on a green candy cane. It was the middle of summer, must have found a discontinued box at a Big Lots or something. Bottle of jojoba oil, dumped on the hood of the car, sizzling in the Midwest sun — I think I applied it liberally to bring out the luster in the paint, but maybe it was a goof. The department store's brown-red brick walls radiated and ebbed heat like the lava rocks in a cheap gas grill. I could feel the warmth from three dozen feet away.

I watched a man in Bermuda shorts, black socks, and sandals scream at a kid at the loading dock for not doing his job right. There's an old man yelling on the back of the state quarter, nothing unusual there. He'd bought a chest freezer big enough to hold six adult bodies (and I'm talking corn-fed midwestern adults, not like anorexic runway models) and he wanted it loaded in the back seat of his subcompact sedan. The kid, who obviously never played much Tetris, was trying to angle and navigate the giant box into the rear door. I almost wanted to go help him, but never get involved. You never want to get involved...

* * *

A month or ten later... got to traffic court at six AM, took the whole day off work to try to beat this bullshit speeding ticket... I mean, it wasn't bullshit; I was technically going 40 or 50 over the limit, blew right past that marked cop car, and they clocked me dead to rights... at least they couldn't nail me for sleeping... It was bullshit because I had to appear in traffic court at six AM, assume the position... explained to the judge that my religious condition prohibited fines and fees... He was too busy swiping through Grindr profiles on his phone to listen. I'm flop-sweating to death, trying to quote *Board of Education of Westside Community Schools v. Mergens (1990)* because I found it in a meme, and the dude's moaning to pictures of some personal trainer/rent boy, about to jizz under the bench...

Prosecutor got bored with me, dropped the charges down to nine MPH over the limit, maximum fines but no license suspension or mandatory driving school. At least I got that goin for me. Almost stuck around to watch the trial for a guy who drove his car through a Walmart on a coke bender after watching *The Blues Brothers*, but I knew it would go on forever and then get delayed a week. I wanted to pay the piper and get the hell out of there.

I swear the clerk in the office was the secretary from *Ferris Bueller's Day Off,* but it couldn't have been the same woman. Maybe her sister. Maybe they cloned them all in a secret government lab in Idaho. She painted her monstrous nails with a polish that smelled like lacquer car finish and ignored me, even when I waved around a wad of cash like an NBA player at a Vegas strip club. The office looked like a World War II bunker, institutional lead paint on the walls a hundred layers thick, old steam radiators hissing like *Eraserhead* in the middle of March. Seventy-two degrees outside, and the boiler's working overtime, the chambers a balmy hundred and seventeen degrees. Must have been some law passed by the coal industry, who knows.

She made me pay the fee in cash, no checks or credit cards accepted. I peeled off a stack of one-dollar bills from the fat roll I kept hidden in an air vent in my basement, slapped them out one-by-one, wasting even more of their time. The lady made me audibly count the bills three more times, and I wondered if her husband fucked her once a year with an empty Avon cologne bottle in the shape of a race car or light house. I don't know, maybe she fucked him. It's the twentieth century, why not. I could barely read the carbon copy of the tissue-thin yellow legal form, but kept the copy for my records, as indicated by the fine print.

A weird old man in a thick robe like a Jedi sat in the waiting area, crying and beating his chest like a religious freak in the middle ages. I tried to ignore him... no time for someone else's sorrow. "THIS WILL BE ON YOUR PER-MANENT RECORD!" he yelled. He pulled out a tambourine with rusty metal zils, and beat it against his head while waving his arms in a little jig. "THIS WILL BE ON YOUR PERMANENT RECORD! PERMANENT! PER-MANENT! PERMANENT! WE ARE ALL IN THEIR COMPUTERS NOW! GOD DAMN THE IN-TERNATIONAL BUSINESS MACHINES CORPORA-TION! DAMN THEIR PERMANENT RECORD! FUCK BILL GATES!"

* * *

Freedom... I found a Church's Chicken next to an abandoned high school, which once had the claim to fame that the third replacement bass player for Alice in Chains once puked in their men's room. It was a rogue Church's that only sold fried chicken, biscuits, and bags of potato chips. Open twenty-four hours, but no breakfast items available. No french fries, no okra, no slaw. Definitely no jalapeño cheese bombers at this location. I ordered a large drink, and sat in a faded plastic booth, contemplating my options. It was only 6:47 AM on a Friday morning. I could go to work, or I could tell them on Monday that the court was jammed and it took all day, which seemed like a better idea.

"I HAVE MEMORIZED ALL CHURCH'S LOCA-TIONS!" An off-duty cashier sat in a booth by the trash cans, chewing on discarded chicken wings, cracking the bones with his deformed dinosaur teeth. He wore a boys' suit and looked like an alt-right disaster. He asked me if I'd ever tried this Panera rip-off restaurant called "Soup and Shit." "THEY'VE GOT SOME GOOD BREAD THERE, IT'S ALL BAKED WITHIN A WEEK OF USE. CHECK THEIR DUMPSTER IF YOU DON'T BELIEVE ME. YOU COULD EAT LIKE A KING FROM THE DUMPSTERS OF THIS GREAT NATION. SERIOUSLY, CHECK OUT THEIR BREAD. HELL OF A LOT BETTER THAN THIS PLACE, BUT THEY WON'T HIRE ME. WHAT KIND OF FAST FOOD JOINT TESTS YOUR PISS? IT'S NOT LIKE I'M FLYING A PLANE, LET ME SMOKE METH IN PEACE. IT'S NON-ADDICTIVE, TOTALLY NOT BAD FOR YOU AT ALL. FREE COUNTRY, LAST TIME I CHECKED."

Again with the yelling. At least this wasn't an old man on Social Security who wouldn't shut up about the evils of socialism. I fondled the little indentations in the top of the cup, the ones the cashier pushed to denote that the soda is diet, root beer, 7-Up, etc. Because of the proliferation of various diet and fruit combinations, the cup had something like a million possible little bumps to encode an entire short story in braille, or a JPEG image of up to 72K. I had a cursory knowledge of braille (tried dating a blind girl for a minute in college, don't ask), so I started entering lines from Homer's *Odyssey* in the bubbles while the guy yelled about how crank cured cancer. This would make the perfect public access TV show, if the guy was smart enough to run a camcorder, which he was not. Maybe he could start a podcast.

Kept thinking about that guy in the robe at the county courthouse. He looked like a friend of my dad's, an old Army buddy who quit his job as a postal worker to start a corn-based religion out in Iowa or Idaho or one of those square states filled with nothing but farms and Shoney's. This was during the middle of that big personal improvement fad in the early Eighties, when people first learned about aerobics and the power of positive thinking. There was a lot of cash in false prophets that year, and this guy was no exception. He gave up government retirement and health care to go door-to-door, telling people to worship corn. This was after the 1973 Farm Act started paying farmers to grow corn, but long before corn got out of control, became Big Corn, and got its own hand-wringing Netflix documentary. So maybe he was on to something.

This friend of my dad's, I think his name was Darrell or Dale or something — we visited him once, on an endless road trip to an amusement park in Dallas owned by a local mega-church. The park was themed after the Trail of Tears, and was very anti-Native American, pro-Indian Removal Act. College kids dressed like Andrew Jackson walked around the concourse, selling ice cream and simulated smallpox blankets. The owners were horribly racist, always appearing on right-wing radio programs to talk about white supremacy, new theme park rides, and the buy 9/get one at 10% off hot dogs.

After filing bankruptcy or going to prison or something, they sold the whole thing to the Chinese, and in the Nineties, the property was turned into a *My Little Pony*-themed park. That ran okay for a year or two, then went to seed after the first big *MLP* wave. It got shut down a decade later because of all the public sodomy and sex acts committed between Bronys. Also the park was way overpriced, and only had Pepsi products and no good rides, just a slow Ferris wheel and bumper cars you had to pay extra for.

Anyway, when we visited Darrell or Dale or whatever, he was holed up in a compound made out of a dozen single-wide trailers, the ends cut off and the whole collection welded together into a large continuous circle, almost like the centrifuge of the spaceship from *2001: A Space Odyssey*, but with a lot more rust. Plenty of space for guests, but the whole interior echoed too much and made sleeping impossible. Didn't smell too great, either. He fed us nothing but corn for three days straight: on the cob, creamed, steamed, in bread form, even in soup, which was almost as disgusting as putting spaghetti in chili.

"I can't get rid of this shit," he told us, while ladling cold corn surprise from a large pot into Dixie paper bowls he bought in bulk. "I thought corn farming would be the greatest swindle, and now I'm fucked. I've got corn up the ass here, both figuratively and literally. I never should have left the government. At least I had a solid three non-corn meals a day, out digging ditches for The Man. Pension, paid breaks, real insurance. I've got buddies at the post office who haven't shown up for work in ten years, and they're still drawing checks. Other than the food stamps I sell to my neighbor, I haven't seen one thin dime out of this bullshit."

Our family lost touch with Darrell/Dave after the disillusioning trip. I think he later killed himself, or maybe he's in prison for fraud. His wife — I think it was his wife, it could have just been one of those groovy key party/cult leader fuck-frenzy trips — popped up in the news, years later, trying to pay a South Korean genetics lab to clone her iguana collection. I don't remember if they did it or not, just that her story caught air in a slow news cycle, right-wing pundits bitching about how cloning was in the bible and people should maybe start firebombing her house. It dropped out of the news fast — it was right before the President said he was attaching the nuclear missile launch button to a Ouija board — and I can't find a wikipedia page on her, or on reptile cloning.

Finished my soda, and it was just after seven in the morning. I guess I could drive to the mall and sleep in my car for three hours. I honestly didn't know there was an iguana shortage. Don't they eat those down in Mexico? Wasn't there a Wall of Voodoo song about this?

The Bat Boy McRib Iron Lung

The used car salesman's armpits were bleeding profusely. Everyone at church thought it was the stigmata, and a deacon called the *Weekly World News*. Turned out it was lymph node cancer, but the 'News still sent a reporter, put a Bat Boy mask on the dude, and wrote a fake article about how he had sex with Bill Clinton in a fallout shelter.

* * *

The new Scorsese movie about the McRib was six hours long, so they had a fifteen-minute intermission at the halfway point. When I stumbled into the lobby to take a piss, a group of vegan protestors were throwing bags of human shit into the auditorium. There were no employees to clean it up, since the theater only had one person working, and he had to run the projectors for all twelve screens, take tickets, sell concessions, and valet park cars. At least it was mostly solid shit, like a three on the Bristol stool scale. Vegans eat a lot of fiber.

* * *

I met someone at the piano store who claimed he was one of the last people in an iron lung. "I played water polio as a kid. Now I can't breathe anymore." He said he could spend up to an hour a day out of the machine, so he'd go to stores downtown and shoplift, because it was the perfect alibi. He had a gym bag full of sheet music, and wanted me to run distraction so he could haul out a concert grand piano when nobody was looking. He could barely breathe while at rest; maybe he could grab a Casio mini-keyboard and make it? No idea. And I didn't want to be the one who told him iron lungs were for polio, not polo.

Krogermania!

...Another dream about working at a Kroger with Ed Gein, watching him chop apart human bodies straight from the grave on the stainless-steel Hobart back in the butcher department. Formaldehyde dust clouds in the air from all that embalmed flesh made everyone in the back of the store loopy, drunk on sherm. I mopped the floors of flesh juice and made crazy prank announcements on the intercom. Dial 7-7 on any phone in the store, and you're an instant performer. All the world's a stage, or at least every speaker in the joint. Back before Shitbook, this was your biggest opportunity as an entertainer, next to maybe lucking out with Ed McMahon's *Star Search*.

"Attention Kroger shoppers! We're splitting the atom back in the pharmacy department! Free thermonuclear warhead with each prescription you fill. Limit twelve per customer, due to the SALT II treaty! Also, it's April 3rd — celebrate the death of former provisional president of Chile Alfredo Duhalde Vásquez with a 144-pack of corn dogs in the freezer section. A replica of the 1966 black Ford Galaxie XL Convertible used as the Chilean presidential vehicle will be on display this Saturday, courtesy of Lockmondy Ford! And don't forget some Kroger-brand ranch dressing for those corn dogs! Made with real artificial buttermilk! Available in 55-gallon drums in Aisle 7!"

Did I already tell you the story about the time I went to a Mexican rodeo in a Kroger? Glenn Danzig was there, of course. He wasn't competing; he was eating cake and trying to get someone to punch him in the head again so he could show that he could take it and was no god damned son of a bitch. There was a Weird Al tribute band playing, and the singer looked like the old Weird Al with the glasses and curly hair, but was hispanic. They played all Weird Al parodies, but they played parodies of the parodies, which you'd think would be just the original songs, but it's not like a photocopy of a photocopy gives you a perfectly clear image. (And no, they did not play parodies of any of his non-parody songs, which is too bad, because I think his best song is "Dare to Be Stupid," which is more of a Devo style parody.) Also the songs were all in Ranchera style, or Mariachi or whatever it's called.

I wanted to find a bull rider who could explain to me the allure of the whole thing, because I was writing a zine and needed something other than record reviews and long lists of everything I ate for lunch over the course of the last ten years. The only person who would talk to me had been kicked in the head an hour ago, and I could see gray matter oozing from his ears and the top of his skull. He told me a story about how his dad rode those little shriner motorcycles in parades professionally for thirty-five years, and he thought riding bulls was a step up, because you only have to work like eight seconds a week, and you didn't have to wear a little hat. I asked him if he worried about brain damage, but he was too busy trying to mop up his cerebrospinal fluid leakage with a *Yo! MTV Raps* beach towel.

One thing I will tell you about rodeos: they always have an impressive snack bar, especially if you're a fat fuck like me who likes to shove fried food in their piehole constantly. Just saying "Mexican rodeo" makes me gain five pounds. I must have hate-fucked ten thousand calories of deep-fried something-or-other drenched in nacho cheese without even thinking. And Mexican Coke, of course. Sucked down at least ten of those little glass bottles of sugar syrup and didn't even notice. Fried Snickers bars for days, and I don't even know what meat they were putting in their chimichangas, but I deep-throated at least five of them, with extra sour cream. Fuck the USDA food pyramid, and live in the now.

In the dream, Gein lectured me on the importance of family, after I went on a tirade about how my mom was driving me nuts with her usual satanic panic anti-video game thing. She took away my Nintendo, and he was trying to tell me she cared about my well-being, or some stupid shit. I didn't know at the time that Ed kept his mom's dead body in his farmhouse and spent his nights running around in a dead skin suit made from the corpses of elderly women he necro-fucked. I ignored him regardless. Never take advice from a butcher. Even butchering advice. Never take advice from anybody, but especially butchers.

* * *

...Standing in a Kroger, trying to buy a cake, and of course the bakery clerk won't shut up. "Hey, was that band Train about trains? Like did they sing songs about locomotives and cabooses and tunnels and stuff? Or was it model trains? Neil Young owns Lionel Trains now, that could be it." The woman working at the grocery store cake department had ridiculously large breasts, and I wondered if it was a hormonal imbalance, or if someone on the internet paid for the implant surgery in exchange for videos of her wearing a sheer bra and shaving her armpits in HD quality. I found that web site one night and could never unsee it. "I know they had a song on *One Tree Hill* — you ever watch that show? Chad Michael Murray is so dreamy. I could listen to him sing about trains every day and never get bored of it. I don't care if I know nothing about trains."

All I wanted was to order a cake for The Firestorm, and I had to listen to this top-heavy minimum wage baker ramble on for an hour straight about bad jam bands of the Nineties and third-rate TV shows nobody in their right mind ever watched. I stared at her moon-shaped Midwestern face while she babbled, and tried to determine if she was thin-fat or fat-thin. The Kroger smock hid most of her vital features, but she must have had a 58-30-48 figure. I also couldn't determine if she was like 20 or 50. It could go either way.

At this point in my dating life, I didn't care, it didn't matter. Her obsession with crappy teen shows on The WB network would normally have been a deal-breaker worse than ten kids and a psychologically unstable husband with an extensive gun collection and a drinking problem, but at this point, I'd even overlook that. She did have nice hair. And she smelled like cake, which was a plus.

There was precedent to this. Back in the day, I knew a grocery store bakery person, although she wasn't at Kroger — maybe Marsh or IGA, I forget. One time I was sick with a respiratory infection, high fever, delirious and talking to my roommate about how Boca Raton had been colonized by aliens and they were infecting people's subconscious thought by adding phantom code to the IBM OS/2 operating system. (It did ship on like 254 floppy disks, so it's possible there was some extraneous stuff in there.) It was my birthday, but I was in no shape to interact with humans. The baker friend called, and when she heard about the birthday, she said she'd be right over.

She swung by my pad with a botched abortion cake — I mean, it wasn't a cake laced with RU-486 that caused spontaneous abortion; it said "congratulations on your abortion, Judy!" but the people ordering it wanted it for Jody, and they couldn't scrape the letters off and change it because of some bullshit health department reason. (I am not a cake artist, I don't know why. Maybe it has to do with frosting cross-contamination or something.) Instead of throwing it in the garbage, she brought it over and I ate the entire sheet cake while watching every Laura Dern movie I could rent on VHS. (*Wild at Heart* is probably the best, even though I got in an argument with Barry Gifford during the 1995 MLB playoffs once, and swore I would never buy any more of his books, although I don't remember what the argument was about. I also like that one movie where she huffs spray paint. The dinosaur thing is ok, but no tits.)

This was one of those situations where I was madly in love with the cake woman, but thought I had no chance, and then ten years later, after she was married with kids, she told me I totally had the green light back then, and she dropped hints constantly, and of course I had no idea. Like even if her hints were bringing me a sheet cake while I was sick and literally telling me, "hey, we should probably fuck, no strings attached," I still didn't get it. Anyway, she left the bakery game long before, and I had no other hookup in the pastry world. So here I was, trying to negotiate with a woman who I either despised or desperately wanted, depending on the flickering of the lighting in the store.

"Look," I told the cashier. "This is a custom job. Your off-the-shelf office party/promise ceremony cakes aren't going to cut it. I need a cake that's all black inside, with black frosting and black edges, and then put black flowers on it, and black lettering. I'm willing to pay up to six dollars extra."

"I don't know if you really want that," she said. "To be honest, it's going to turn your poo bright black for days."

"That's exactly why I want to do it," I said. "None more black."

"Okay, it's your cake. What do you want it to say?"

"I need it to say 'Oh hail Satan, Yes hail Satan, it's a Black Firestorm' in letters that are as big as possible. And as tall as possible. Like stack the frosting a foot high."

"Oh, I'm not sure I can do that. I'm not comfortable making any Satanic cakes. It's the law." She pointed to a sign on the wall, which said the state allowed the shop to refuse service to Satanists or anyone who owned an Iron Maiden album. "It says 'Satanists' right there. State law."

"Well, can you just make a blank cake and I'll buy my own frosting and freehand the lettering myself?"

"No, I'm not comfortable with that, either. You shouldn't have told me you were a Satanist. I'm going to have to ask you to leave the premises after I take a polaroid picture of you and put it on the wall behind the register so nobody ever serves you again."

Fuck it. I won't make a cake this Firestorm. If I was still in the Northeast, maybe I could buy a box of Drake's Devil Dog cakes and call it a day. But in the Midwest, good luck. This was a state that banned the Atari 2600 because Jerry Falwell said it was Satanic. I couldn't even buy bottled water on Sundays without driving over to the next state. I needed to either move, die, or learn how to bake my own fucking cakes.

I Blame My Email Spam on George Ratterman

Someone emailed my Gmail account and said he had to set the record straight on why he missed 87 days of work and gained 200 pounds eating Nutter Butter cookies. (I get a lot of wrong number emails, whatever you want to call it.) His essay went on for fifteen pages and described how his mom vanished and turned up working as a lighting technician under an assumed name on Alice Cooper's European tour back in the seventies.

I remember the line "My genetic disposition for food addiction is no excuse for robbing a football helmet factory when I was twelve, and I'd like to note that there's still a great amount of shame involved, which I can never change."

I emailed him back and asked if he could get me a deal on one of the new football helmets with a built-in radio receiver so the coach can talk to the quarterback. The email bounced, and a week later, two FBI agents showed up to talk to me about my internet searches. I told them I didn't speak English.

Hepatitis is a Growth Industry

Meat tree... Meat tree... Meet tree... Floating, ambient, almost awake. Remembering a distant argument with a shop teacher about the validity of guard rails on highway switchbacks in the mountains... he was anti-guard, but this was a flat state, elevation zero, no hills whatsoever. Guard rails were a complete waste of metal in corn country. Even the idea of gentle hills and a slight curve in the road was an abstract concept here. He was also an Army National Guard sniper on the weekends, and a bit of a flat-earther, too lazy to calculate angle of descent every time he took a long shot. Aim for the head, hit them in the balls, I guess. Myself, I'm a bit too skittish around no rails on a steep curve. I've watched Road Runner cartoons. I know the physics.

...Something about a reality TV show where people collect medical waste, I forget the point of it, maybe trying to get rare finds like antique heart valves and nuclear-powered pacemakers? It's probably based on *Fight Club*, where they dumpster-dove for liposuctioned fat. Two overweight dudes in bowling shirts with ironic beards went from grave to grave with a shovel, and argued about getting a set of fake tits with the lowest serial numbers, like they were trying to get a matching-numbers 1969 Z-28 Camaro at auction.

Endless commercials for the new DNA treatment for hepatitis... I guess people with liver disease must be the target market of the show. The disclaimer read at rapid speed at the end of the commercial mentioned pissing blood and blue discharge from your eyeballs, which didn't sound good. Explains the person I saw puking a stream of what I thought was Hi-C juice at the Arby's last week. (Luckily I got my car washed immediately afterwards.) I couldn't catch the rest of the legal jargon in the commercial without a VCR that did 8x slo-mo, but they said to see their ad in this month's *Golf Digest*.

...Time to go shopping, just like George Bush told me to. Thought about pulling over and getting a room at a business hotel between my house and the Guitar Center — 45-minute drive, but I felt so tired, lethargic. Maybe I had lead poisoning. It almost felt worth it to pay a hundred bucks for an anonymous bed, a few hours of free cable TV. No, that's stupid. They never have good cable channels anyway. Last time I spent a week at a Marriott, the twelve channels of TV were all news, except a Mexican bowling channel and a religious thing that only played clips of high-speed car accidents and public beheadings. I was so damn bored, I almost read the bible. (Instead, I tore out the pages of Leviticus about butt sex and wrote "OK BOOMER" on the inside front cover.)

For some reason, the town only allowed smoking inside the Guitar Center, so folks from miles around came there to light up. The inside of the store smelled like a Vegas casino from 1957 during an RJ Reynolds tobacco convention. A thick layer of tar and nicotine coated every stringed instrument hung on the walls. No price reductions, of course. I cruised the pre-owned section for deals, and there were none. Beaten Fenders with the Eddie Van Halen tape stuck on them by toothless idiots, worn and fucked beyond any use, but only marked down ten dollars from the MSRP of a brand new model.

I wanted to buy a Boss Metal Zone pedal so I could record a perfect death metal album by turning every knob towards hell, but their only one in stock looked like it had survived the bus accident that killed Cliff Burton. Also I don't know how to play guitar. I thought about buying a synthesizer controller of some sort, so I could just press buttons and make music, but every time I touch a keyboard, I think about Trent Reznor videos, then that episode of *Friends* where Ross played synthesizer, and I realize it would be a bad idea.

Dream Journal #863

I hooked up with this cheerleader from my high school. Maybe she wasn't a cheerleader (I never went to the damn games) but she was in the in crowd, Fellowshit of Christian Athletes, Izod sweaters, and so on. She always looked older than the rest of the kids, like she was 36 back in high school. It reminded me of the "kids" in a sitcom that take nine seasons to go through four grades.

I was home from college for the summer and mowing my parents' lawn with a Slayer-brand lawn mower and she came over with a 99-can case of Pabst Blue Ribbon and was trying to get me drunk so I would fix her computer. I sipped one beer while she chugged eleven and she was suddenly my best friend, flirting and sitting far closer to me than my social standing would dictate. She went to the same big dumb state university as me and wondered why we never ran into each other on campus, or why we didn't hit it off in high school. I didn't explain to her that we never even talked in high school, and I never go to jock bars or talk to anyone.

She passed out, and while I was mowing the rest of the lawn, my friend Lars showed up, performed exploratory surgery on her, and perfectly closed her back up with polyfilament fishing line. We drove to the 7-Eleven with her body strapped to the hood of his giant Chrysler car. I asked him when he learned surgical techniques, and he told me they taught it at the mail-order diesel mechanics school he did for a semester as a joke. We left her at the gas station before she woke up, and I bought a twenty-five pound crate of Slim Jims so I could mail away for the full-size Randy Savage doll.

Wyoming Does Not Exist

America is nothing but a Slim Jim delivery system for the gun-toting morbidly obese. I'd been driving around rural Kansas or Wyoming or some other cowboy state for hours, looking for a place that would let me connect to the internet at faster than 2400 baud. (And yes, I realize there is a difference between baud and bits per second, but there's no difference when you're talking about a slow signal rate and a modem that's older than a World War One battleship, so stop being so fucking pedantic.) The only thing I found were Wal-Marts, churches, churches made out of Wal-Marts, Wal-Marts in churches, and churches where people worship Wal-Marts. I thought I found an iPhone repair shop that may have had an internet cafe terminal in it, but when I went inside, it was an anti-iPhone shop selling Wal-Mart phones. A bunch of old people in 18th-century church clothes prayed at an effigy of Sam Walton and burned their electronics as a sacrifice to their master. They didn't even sacrifice real iPhones; they were so cheap, they used the fake plastic demonstration phones Wal-Mart put in store displays for phone cases.

This was the point in time where I thought Wyoming didn't exist. I'd never met anyone from Wyoming. Never visited there, never had a reason to visit there. Maybe I flew over the Cowboy State going from Chicago to Seattle, but with the curvature of the earth, maybe not. This was before the rich and famous from Hollywood and Silicon Valley were buying up property in Jackson Hole, commuting by Lear jet to their million-square-foot "cabins" to show people they were grounded, real-world folk, while a staff of twenty cooked five-course macrobiotic gourmet meals. I think the most famous person actually from Wyoming was John Eugene Osborne, and I'm sure unless you are a political science major who writes a lot of papers about state politics in 1893, he doesn't exist. Wyoming didn't exist. Even after I drove through it for hours, I was still certain it didn't exist. I don't think I even exist. I wrote a book about this one time.

Thermonuclear war could do this area some good, I thought. A nice air-blast of a 25-megaton warhead would work wonders for the real estate market. I fantasized about a Soviet R-36M (SS-18 Mod 3) rocket with a single high-throw warhead streaking in from a trip across the North Pole and ending my misery. The only problem with daydreaming about all-out nuclear war during a long drive across nothingness is that I'd eventually pull out my phone and start researching how much the MX missile program cost and become depressed that we spent so much money (something like $20 billion in 1980s dollars for 114 missiles) and never got to launch any of the things. They could have at least taken out some old shopping malls or a Vegas casino instead of just scrapping the missiles outright, or maybe launched them in a Fourth of July show. Make it a pay-per-view, earn back a few bucks of that money. At least the Russians got to use their missiles in parades. We paid billions of dollars for the Peacekeeper missile program and didn't even get to look at one, except in video games and music videos.

I knew a woman in college obsessed with the MX missile, like so much you couldn't even talk about Mexican food around her or she'd start on a diatribe. She studied cable gender studies, read a lot of Andrea Dworkin, and claimed all ballistic missiles were some penis envy thing, which is probably true, although I didn't want to admit to her that she was right about anything. She worked at the popcorn stand in the student union, which was in the same part of the concourse as a bunch of arcade machines thrown in a random room, a makeshift arcade for the terminally bored and addicted. That was me. I had a real problem one semester with the game *Golden Axe*, and spent an entire Pell grant twenty-five cents at a time trying to beat a GA machine in that arcade, so I ran into her a lot, and we became casual acquaintances.

The woman — I don't remember her name, Susan or Sharon or something, looked like a member of the Manson family who wasn't cool enough to go on the murder sprees and was left behind to cook breakfast, only to later go frumpy and end up spending twenty years trying to finish an undergraduate sociology degree while selling greasy popcorn a bag at a time. I had a love/hate relationship with popcorn

— empty calories, irresistible smell, bad dental trauma. I couldn't eat it, but couldn't not eat it. Luckily the ever-flowing stream of evil minions of the Death Adder kept me too busy to shove too much air-popped into my stupid giant head.

"You know all computers are sexist," she told me one afternoon, after I ran out of tokens. "It's why computers only have female cable connectors on them. They're implying females are objects for breeding for cock-oppressor cables. And computer memory is measured in bytes because they're fat-shaming women who eat too much."

"Tell that to Werner Buchholz of IBM. He coined the term." I knew correcting her would mean my house would get firebombed by militant lesbians, but I only rented, and had no skin in the real estate game. Becoming temporarily homeless and losing all my worldly possessions could be a good thing. As long as she didn't force me to read Camille Paglia, I would be fine.

"Video games are even more sexist. Name a video game with a female protagonist. And Ms. Pac-Man doesn't count — they just put a bow on Pac-Man to sell more copies. Plus that game reinforces negative dietary standards, and is offensive to spiritual belief systems."

"*Golden Axe*! I just played it for two hours straight! One of the three playable characters is the amazon Tyris Flare!"

"You spent two hours playing a video game where you're an amazon warrior?"

"No, I played as Gilius Thunderhead. He's a dwarf with a battle axe. Tyris has better magical ability, but Gilius starts with more strength."

"Sexist, just as I thought. You should really consider going to class instead of playing that game all day."

She was right, but I wasn't going to admit it. Three straight semesters of no academic progress, and I was still staying awake until eight in the morning and sleeping all day. I'd later regret this, but I'd later regret pretty much everything I'd do with my life, including writing this piece of shit story and driving across Wyoming, which didn't exist.

Roll The Bones Is My Favorite Gangsta Rap Album

- Someone screaming "Jesus take the wheel!" right before driving their car off a bridge.

- Two people arguing over whether or not the salt at Wendy's or McDonald's tastes better.

- A competitive diarrhea blog that hasn't been updated since 2014.

- Someone skydiving into an alligator farm to remake that *Faces of Death* scene for TikTok.

- Kim Jong Il is still alive, working as a fry cook in a Cracker Barrel in Wichita, Kansas.

- A riot during a table tennis competition at the local YMCA where fourteen players are beheaded.

- MC Hammer spent all of his record money on Lionel train sets. He was secretly a big Neil Young fan.

- The GoPro Hero9 camera is not for rectal use.

Sewage Beach

The beach smelled like raw sewage, a thick, fermented stench of pure death. Every fifty feet, signs erected by the local tourism board humble-bragged about the outstanding quality of their locally sourced excrement. I think it was some kind of new-age thing, *e coli* for weight loss, the Raw Sewage Movement. Big Sanitation wants to throw around their money cleaning natural probiotics out of our drinking water; nobody back in the fourteenth century purified their waste, and they had no school shootings whatsoever. It was the usual scam, and Whole Foods would be selling bottles of straight-up human shit for twenty dollars each within weeks. Go to Etsy and get the latest in homemade small-batch blackwater sewage drinks.

I recognized the cove in a distant déjà vu vision of the past, a mirage of a time when I drank cheap rum by the gallon and chased whores like there was no tomorrow. I had a roommate named Curtis back in college that majored in some obscure beach management program, one of those academic pseudo-departments heavily funded by a covert CIA program that threw millions of dollars into a field of study only usable for Normandy-style coastal invasions of Caribbean Islands whose neo-communist regimes had long since been overthrown by casinos and fast food companies. When he wasn't tripped out on his daily regimen of shrooms and trying to fuck a Grateful Dead record, Curtis preached a lot about erosion and beach design, and I picked up bits of it through osmosis. (And no, he wasn't fucking the 9/32" hole in an LP. He drilled them out to a typical glory hole size. This only made the Grateful Dead albums sound worse, as they lolled around the turntable platter off-center.)

In his usual psilocybin haze, Curtis often described meticulous coves and quarries he designed in some piece-of-shit proprietary DOS program that was used to draw coastlines using ASCII letters and symbols. "Infinity swimming pools are the work of the devil," he told me, as we stumbled through the school art museum, making fun of everything in sight and looking for a place to day drink. (This was a dry campus, but some of the art openings and exhibits could get a waiver to serve champagne or wine. One time we were trespassing around the hotel connected to the student union and stumbled into an abortion vacuum cleaner convention. We managed to steal a full-size catering pan of beanie weenies that were set out in a steam table and forgotten.)

"Anything other than an above-ground you can buy at Sears is cheating, plain and simple. And it's a big red flag, honestly." MFA student exhibits surrounded us like a maze of torment, fiber arts monstrosities and ugly ceramics with bullshit conceptual artists' statements about the plight of the dolphins. And no alcohol whatsoever. "We all know any high-demand structural engineering project originating in

France is just a boondoggle invented to promote the Roth-schild banks. Think about it. I'm all for french fries, french toast, and french whores, but the French swimming pool construction industry is a death cult waiting to infect us all. I AM AN AMERICAN!"

I did think about it, for about five seconds, and then a girl in acid-washed jorts with the ass of an angel walked past, and his half-baked conspiracy theory completely vanished, my brain a floppy disk held against a 10,000-gauss junkyard electromagnet used to pick up cars. I smiled, said hello, but it's always useless. After she faded from view, the thought of the ASCII-art coves haunted me, something about the ratio of the curves in contrast to the shore. I could understand why Curtis kept talking about lighthouses so much, in an almost sexual fashion. Long after he died in an unfortunate fisting accident at an Arbor Day celebration in 1989, I won-dered if anything he said was true, or if it was all a figment of my imagination, somehow warped by golden ratio math-ematical nonsense I couldn't consciously fathom.

"Hey man, you want to buy an iced kombucha?" Outside the art museum, a guy with smelly white boy dreads running wild like Medusa pulled a little red wagon with an Igloo cooler filled with homemade beverages that looked like the poison a warrior would drop from a castle turret during siege warfare. Smelled like it too. "Only ten dollars. It's probiotic. Contains a billion active counts."

"Counts of what?"

"Um, counts of probiotic. Calories? Vitamins? Something, I don't know. It's good for you. Promotes cancer. I mean, cancer-free, you know? Ten bucks. Three for fifty. You wanna party?"

Curtis asked if they had booze in them, and the guy couldn't say yes or no. I'm sure there was like half a percent of alcohol content and if you drank like fifteen of them, you'd start to cop a buzz, but if you drank that much fermented tea, you'd be both bankrupt and in need of a complete digestive system transplant, so no. We'd pick up a sixer of the cheapest thing possible at the gas station and drink it warm.

On the walk home, Curtis told me some story about taking eight hundred hits of acid that week, seeing *The Lion King*, and inventing guitar sweep-picking. This was dozens of years after all of those shred guitar guys from the Eighties, so I had no idea where he was going with this. I also ended up buying us both Domino's pizza for some reason.

* * *

I barely knew our fifth roommate, an accounting major from Calumet City who allegedly had a girlfriend back home, but I was thinking he concocted this story so people wouldn't bother him about his asexuality. He looked like a young, more socially awkward John Hinckley, and always wore sweater vests, even when it was a hundred degrees out. This was before every third person in generation Z self-identified as having Asperger's, and my only reference to autism was the movie *Rain Man*, so I'm not going to say he was on the spectrum, but you get the idea here.

We called him Chuck, but I'm not sure if that was his actual name. I wouldn't be surprised if his legal name was something completely different, and someone had called him Chuck by accident and it stuck because he was too polite to correct them. And I couldn't verify this by his mail, because either he didn't believe in the USPS, or he got everything delivered to his parents. Maybe both.

We rented this big oddball house with five bedrooms and two half-baths. Chris and Brenda shacked in one bedroom, and me and Curtis each had our own microhotel-sized room. The other two bedrooms were computer offices where we dumped our various tech gear, and they were always boiler room hot from simultaneously running a dozen different ancient tower-sized Pentium machines. Chuck slept in a closet in the back, actually more of a utility room that was unheated and maybe used to be a back porch that was sealed up in the Sixties with spare plywood, and converted into an illegal bedroom.

I distinctly remember only one conversation with Chuck, about the Toledo War. This was an actual armed conflict in 1835 between Ohio and the Michigan territory over a tiny strip of land maybe a mile or two wide near the Maumee River, going from Toledo to the Indiana border. I don't know how this happened, except maybe land surveying wasn't an exact science in the Nineteenth century. Chuck was writing a role-playing game about the incident, which sounded almost as boring as studying accounting. He explained to me how Michigan gave up the chunk of land in exchange for the upper peninsula, which maybe was a fair trade, but I never understood how you could have a state that's made of two pieces, even though I lived in Michigan for like seven years once.

I didn't have much to add to the discussion, so I told him about the time I briefly dated a girl from Toledo in my freshman year of college, and when I visited her parents in Ottawa Hills over Thanksgiving break, she woke me up in the middle of the night and gave me a hand job, which is the most exciting thing that had ever happened to me (or anyone) within the confines of Lucas County. And I guess I went to Tony Packo's and ate hot dogs too. I think I upset him, either because a description of any sex act made him uncomfortable, or maybe he had high hopes for me to play his stupid game. But this was long before RPGs somehow became cool and nerd culture was appropriated. Also, he slightly smelled, like maybe he never used deodorant, and that doesn't go well with wearing a sweater vest and oxford shirt when it's a hundred degrees outside.

By the time me and Curtis got home that afternoon to finish off the last two cans of warm Meister-Brau and our now-cold Domino's pizza of sadness, our roommate Brenda accosted us in the hallway. Brenda was always bent out of shape about something, but that day she seemed particularly unhinged. "Well, this is fucking great — up the rent by 25% each!"

"What, did the landlord finally agree to fix the second toilet?" One of the half-baths had no toilet at all, just a capped-off hole in the floor. The landlord said it was for aesthetic reasons; I think he was just lazy.

"No, Chuck vanished. Completely skipped town. All of his stuff is gone. I called his parents — their name is on the sublease. They haven't seen him in years."

I wondered what two people who fucked to create a monster like Chuck would look like, but I was barely holding down the warm beer, so I didn't want to dwell on this too much. "Maybe he ran off with his girlfriend."

"Yeah, that girlfriend, if she even existed, was like that chick Elton John married in the Eighties. We should probably call the Secret Service, and maybe Jodie Foster's agent, just in case."

* * *

...Must have wandered down to the water in a haze, fell asleep on the sewage beech sand. I awoke to the sound of two junkies fighting each other over a garbage bag full of crushed aluminum cans. One of the addicts was tall, lanky, good reach but covered in sores from skin-popping horse into every greasy, unwashed square inch of his body. The other fighter was a fatbody terminal addict who could shoot smack, smoke crack, snort endless amounts of blow and crank, but still weigh 500 pounds. The beanpole guy got in some good jabs, and I assumed he would win the battle, but the big dude's portly frame took some significant blunt-force trauma, and he wasn't going down. It was like watching a rat try to kill an elephant.

The tide rose while I was asleep, and I was soaking wet, almost drowned in the undercurrent. Not exactly the best smell to have soaked into your clothes. Luckily, back in the car I had an old Hot N' Now Hamburgers t-shirt and some jeans that had been washed so many times, they were a frosty white, like David Coverdale's hair. I also had my emergency bar of Lava soap in my trunk full of contingency garbage I'd never use. After ten minutes of a freezing cold Silkwood shower with the Lava bar in a cabana next to the beach restrooms, I smelled like the chemical goodness of a janitor's supply storeroom, and my skin was on the verge of bleeding from the heavily pumiced soap. But, no sewage stench.

A steep wall of rocks surrounded the beach, leading back to the roadway. The walk up the stone division to my car, back down again to the shower, and up a third time almost killed me, the primitive staircase covered in a green mold, moist with the remains of the morning dew. My plastic-soled imitation army boots slipped and slid on the steps, and I almost fell and broke my arm a thousand times over. As I exfiltrated from the beach, I watched an endless parade of jets soar over the horizon, passing a hundred feet over the sand dunes. The airport sat about a quarter-mile east of the water, and a constant barrage of million-pound cylinders of aluminum and gasoline streaked towards the ocean from the tarmac in the near distance.

This would be the perfect place to camp out with a rocket launcher and take out 747s climbing over the Pacific, I thought. I imagined the scenario, hanging around in a lawn chair with an extra-large bag of Cool Ranch Doritos and a FIM-92A Stinger missile, watching for a jet full of tourists returning home from a long Disneyland excursion. I didn't know how to score a Stinger missile these days — all the ones the CIA left behind in Afghanistan back in the day had dead batteries, allegedly. And the guy I knew at the Dairy Queen in Goshen, Indiana who dealt in this stuff had recently moved to Uruguay to start a salad dressing business. The Doritos sounded like a good idea, though.

My car was one of the only ones left in the parking lot, except for a rusty maroon Oldsmobile Toronado with a dead body in it, a housewife suicide by valium and box wine. Her husband assumed she was on a dick-sucking/outlet mall shopping rampage and didn't call in her disappearance; the authorities wouldn't find her for another few months. Shards of glass from broken bottles of bum wine and lite beer covered the hot asphalt car park. Amber and green chips and slivers glistened in the sunlight, and made me want a drink, a drink of anything to quench the thirst from climbing around the stupid beach.

The driver's seat felt like putting my ass on a vinyl-covered George Foreman grill. I shook the mud out of my combat boots, put my only 8-track tape (ZZ Top — *Eliminator*) into the dash of the car, and drove to the putt-putt golf course across the highway from the state park. The car didn't have air conditioning, and it was so hot inside, the rear-view mirror would fall from the windshield every week, the adhesive boiling away from the intense heat. I ran the dashboard fan on high, which did almost nothing, and swerved the car to affect a small cross-breeze, like a Formula One racer heating their tires before the start of a race, maybe hoping it would knock loose the stale air. It didn't.

* * *

If anyone ever asks, ZZ Top — *Eliminator* is my all-time, all-star, number-one abandoned-island album pick. There's no comparison. Eleven tracks, forty-four minutes and twenty-eight seconds of perfection, it has everything for everyone. It's got the classic ZZ Tex-Mex feel, the southern boogie blues, the hey-remember-the-Eighties nostalgia, and the polished sound and drum synth of dance music. Plus it just rocks.

The videos are cute, I guess. And I don't really want to get into how the writing credits were slightly disputed, or that it's essentially a self-produced Billy Gibbons solo album (with writing help from sound engineer Linden Hudson) and almost all of the drums and bass using drum machines and synth. But they recorded what was essentially a first draft of the album in drummer Frank Beard's basement in Houston before setting foot in the studio in Tennessee, so the whole band was involved at some point. There's a story of Hudson researching every popular song on the radio to determine their speed and deciding that the album should all be recorded at 120 BPM. Another weird story is how they did a single remix of the song "Legs" and most CD pressings replaced the album version with the single version until the 2008 reissue.

I'm not bullshitting about this. I'm serious. I bought the tape when it came out in 1983, and still listen to it to this day. I've had to re-buy a dozen times in various formats — LP, 8-Track, cassette, CD, HDCD, MP3, FLAC, red vinyl, 180-gram vinyl, MiniDisc, DCC, DAT — and I'd buy it a dozen more, because I support them that much. True story.

* * *

Searching for a drink, I stumbled into the mini-golf course and convenience mart, a strange flashback of yesteryear, back when entertainment options were limited, and families had to do something other than stare at a wall of HDTV.

Back in the day, my hometown had a minor tourism racket going on, one of those "Coney Island in *(insert random location here)*" things that ran a hundred years ago and then was mostly torn down and paved over in the Sixties. Any time I saw bad mini-golf, unsafe wooden roller coasters, or heavily fried food on a stick, it was a direct time machine to my youth.

The course by my house as a kid had a prefab steel building containing a pro shop that also sold comic books, skin flicks on VHS, and candy bars. They also ran a campground on the back half, no questions asked. It was the closest place to my subdivision where we could buy soda pop and ice cream while on foot. The owner was a weird guy with traumatic head injury from 'Nam; a piece of a Claymore went straight through his skull when he was trying to jerk off with the tripwire. Every time I went to the shop to buy an Abba-Zabba bar and look at the stroke mags, he'd tell me the same exact story about how Vic Morrow got beheaded by a Huey chopper when they were filming the *Twilight Zone* movie.

I usually feigned interest, because it's hard to find a cash-only mini-golf course that isn't full of wrinkly, obese swingers trying to fuck and suck each other at all hours of the day. I used to play in a mini-golf tournament at a place like that next to a Golden Corral, and every time I went, I'd get disturbed by the grunts and groans of a gang bang at the public above-ground pool, spray-tanned seniors with Florida hair and more moles than the East German Stasi. They tried to get their moneys' worth on their bootleg Viagra before the Corral opened for the early bird. And none of those fuckers wore a hearing aid, so I'd try to putt through the spinning windmill while oldsters screamed "PUT IT IN WHERE? WHO IS IN MY ASS? JUDY, HOLD MY FALSE TEETH!"

Decades later, and this place looked almost identical, including the same type of addled shopkeeper. Maybe it was a job requirement. "Hey man," the owner said, looking up from his well-worn copy of *Nugget* magazine. "You ever hear about how Vic Morrow's fuckin' head got cut off in that *Twilight Zone* movie? It's all on YouTube... looked like a real-life Romero film. His fuckin' head came right off. Drove that chopper right into the ground."

"Do you have anything even remotely resembling a cold drink here? I am fucking dying of thirst. I'd drink an open glass of warm milk, no questions asked, if it cost less than eight dollars." It probably wouldn't — clotted raw milk was the other big health craze that week. Something about the protein-to-calorie ratio cured cancer or high blood pressure or something. It would take ten dozen salmonella deaths before people wised up on that one, switched to pasteurized or moved on to the next pseudoscience fad.

"I'm clean out of everything. I even sold that last bottle of Lipton I had in the back cooler since Eisenhower was President. That Mexican bull-riding convention this week damn near wiped us out. Got tap water to drink, but it's not very cold. God damn nuclear power plant they built over the hill totally fucked up my well water. Always warm, and it gives everyone these goddamn headaches. I don't have a glass, though. Sold the last one on eBay weeks ago. You could use your hand. Shop teachers' drinking fountain."

"Yeah, I guess. Let me use the shitter first." I went back to the bathroom, a three by three closet with a rough-cut hole in the floor, and a bar sink hanging precariously from a tile wall. An insane collection of homoerotic graffiti littered the walls, desperate murals sketched with marker, pleas for men to show up at specific times to get cornholed in anonymity. I turned on the sink's faucet to cover up the sound of my pissing, and a pure brown water gushed from the tap, a stagnant flow that made Flint, Michigan city water look like pure Evian.

I relieved myself into the hole in the ground, didn't even bother turning off the water, and fled. Even though I didn't touch anything with my hands, I'd still need to bathe myself in alcohol, maybe brillo pad myself to scrape away the top two layers of cells, avoid a MRSA death sentence. I would need more Lava soap, maybe a case of it.

"Hey man, come back! I've got Easter candy on sale! Five for four dollars. Peeps, dude. Bite their fuckin' heads off. Like Vic Morrow! He got his fuckin' head lopped off in that *Twilight Zone* movie. Did I tell you about that yet?"

I hated Peeps, even more than I hated myself. When I was a kid, my parents thought I was allergic to chocolate, and instead of bunnies and eggs made of the standard confectionery treat, I got marshmallow garbage and stale off-brand jelly beans, the bullshit candies one normally throws in the garbage after gorging on the good stuff. I think it permanently scarred me, although I do sometimes binge on the actual Jelly Belly brand beans, the Ronald Reagan ones, not because he endorsed them, but because the coloring they use goes straight through my digestive system intact. Nothing like waking up the morning after you eat a pound of cinnamon jelly beans, taking your morning constitutional, and thinking you suddenly developed colon cancer.

* * *

Days later, weeks later, I figured I needed something for PTSD, although I'm sure they'd want to know what one event gave me PTSD, and it was basically my entire life since birth. Called up the number on the back of my insurance card to find an appointment with someone who could prescribe the good stuff, but they found a loophole to avoid offering any mandatory psych coverage by only doing "telemedicine." They ran a hotline where you call an 800 number, navigate an endless phone tree, sit on hold for hours listening to the Toni Basil song "Mickey" on repeat, and then if you can survive that, you eventually talk to a robot that records you for 50 minutes and then charges you a

$25 copay. The AMA did a study on it or something, said it worked — some new mode of therapy, anti-gestalt cognitive earworm regression, I forget the explanation.

I took the money I'd otherwise blow talking to a digital answering machine and gave it to a psychic with monster tits I found in the back of the yellow pages. She was Egyptian or Romanian or something, a thick unibrow and hairy armpits that smelled like rancid hummus, but she sported at least a full DD cup, and always wore low-cut dresses. Ran a clinic in the back of a Sears, in the little mini-compartment where they used to have a dental clinic, before they gave up on that. I had to overdose on Claritin before I went to her office, because the mass amount of dust mites in her wall tapestries and thick carpets meant an almost-instant allergic reaction, but it was still worth it. The first two or three visits were okay, but my insurance company caught on and stopped reimbursing my claims, so I'd probably only last for another session or two before I stopped going and sat around my house shame-eating as a mode of therapy.

* * *

The psychic went on and on about the haunted souls trapped in the A&W bottling factory outside of Galveston, Texas exploding bottles and cans of soda in a spastic fashion, causing gestational diabetes to flow through the groundwater in plumes of despair. "Get a good way to watch the Halley's Comet before it comes back. Telescope glass, coated with olive oil and root beer. It's like an Oakley wraparound for your mind."

I felt a great need to burn up the rest of the session and explain why I missed the last comet. I will surely be dead long before the next one. I can't say it's my greatest regret in life — you're talking to a guy who shorted Apple stock in 2010 — but it pisses me off that I couldn't get my act straight enough in 1986 to at least look up in the sky for ten seconds and see that thing. Oh well, 2061 is just around the corner. Take your vitamins, eat your vegetables. Maybe I can make it.

What was I doing in 1986 that was more important than a once-in-a-lifetime celestial event, aside from listening to *Master of Puppets* twice a day and jerking off constantly to eighties porno mags with full bush and no insertion? Probably something with computers that could have made me money if I stuck with it. In 1992, someone tried to explain C++ to me and I was certain object-oriented programming would be a stupid fad, and I really needed to get into Crystal Pepsi instead.

After my fifty-minute hour with the tarot cards, I wandered the half-dead department store where she ran her astrology clinic. The woman at the window counter tried to sell me Anderson double-panes and a matching sliding-glass patio setup, to make me keep up with the Joneses. I told her my neighbors were all Laotian and were named Vongvilay or Khanthavong, not Jones. She said the windows would pay for themselves, tax credits and energy savings, but I rented a studio apartment the size of a closet, and didn't even have a window. I was thinking more along the lines of buying an Amiga 500 and a treasure trove of vintage pornography, but I don't know anything, didn't know what would fix me. If I did, I wouldn't be writing fiction in an age when 97% of adults only pick up a book when they need to kill an insect and none of their ten guns are nearby.

I considered what Satanic ritual I could perform that would best encapsulate my experience at the bus station on my way home, possibly something that didn't involve buying any accessories or furniture to sacrifice in flames to our unholy master. But a man kept interrupting me, selling candy bars and bibles outside the Taco Bell Express stand across the street that had been firebombed by a radical vegan group a few weeks before. The entire block smelled like burned plastic and charred Meximelts, which made me simultaneously retch and want nachos and cheese. I pondered the best way to move a civil war cannon from coast to coast without dealing with UPS, and wrote my findings in a Trapper Keeper covered in straight-edge punk stickers. There were no real options. There never are.

A plaid warrior in a ragged kilt, his distended balls hanging below the hem line, stopped to tell me I needed to believe in some made-up guy in the sky, a cult scam involving paint-by-numbers or a special salve you could only buy through the mail, but I ignored him. I'm still trying to get rid of a 50-gallon tub of lemon-scented Amway laundry soap that will follow me to my death. He walked out of the bus station and went to a pawn shop across the street, to pick up some dollar CDs of 90s bands that had completely vanished from the public consciousness. For every "Where Are They Now," Third Eye Blind-level group long forgotten but easily remembered, there were a thousand bands nobody could recall, their members now working at Best Buy for minimum wage or sucking dick in the parking lot of a dollar store for glue money.

* * *

I always thought of that astrology psychic because years later I went to a dentist that was nearby her old office. The Sears predictably went under years ago, and was demolished and turned into a fight club arena and evangelical mega-church. *[I originally said meta-church here and considered keeping it, because that's such a cool concept. -Ed]* But I still thought about it every time I went in for more work in the chair.

During one of my laser root canals in what I call my "experimental endodontic procedure" era of 1996-1998, I had a dental technician, an endodontist's assistant actually, who played accordion or tambourine for the Gin Blossoms in their live band for about ten seconds before their lead guitarist shot himself. "I quit music entirely, moved to Russia to become a rabbi. I wasn't Jewish; I just liked the outfits. Didn't talk to anyone for about two years, then started practicing dentistry on stray animals for a while. It gets cold up there, no cable TV, and you aren't going to find a Hobby Lobby up in Siberia to buy some adult coloring books, you know?"

I totally got it. When I was flunking out of college, heavily abusing cooking sherry and mouthwash, I bought a Jackson Pollock paint-by-number kit from an Assyrian political refugee, a groovy guy covered in boils with a long beard and a crew-cut, way before that look became cool with the hipster set. He sold craft supplies door-to-door to support the Gulf War, or maybe he was against it, I can't remember. I thought about loading up some Bob Ross on the TV and trying to paint some landscapes or Slayer album covers, but I never even cracked open the supplies, and threw them in the garbage three moves later, the little plastic bins of paint gone dry. It was bullshit water-soluble paint anyway, hideous, chalky colors with no fumes at all. If you're going to do a hobby in your spare time, at least find one that gets you high.

* * *

I eventually found a convenience store in El Segundo that sold nothing but energy drinks, and bought five cans of an off-brand clone of Monster energy drink with Lon Chaney Jr. on the bottle. The bottle had him dressed as The Wolf Man, and there was actual hair glued on it. It promised to "put some hair on you," and based on the weak adhesive on the package, it probably would.

I chugged three bottles of the noxious fake-fruit drink, and remembered Lon's legal name was Creighton Tull Chaney. I also remember his first wife divorced him for being "sullen." I wasn't as drunken or rambunctious as the junior Chaney, but I did just wake up half-drowned on a beach full of sewage, so who knows how this would turn out for me.

RICHARD NIXON IS PUNK AS FUCK

Lockheed Martin released full pro-edited multi-cam video evidence of the alien/human hybrid breeding program at Groom Lake, and nobody even noticed because the news wasn't written in the form of a Buzzfeed quiz. High-def video footage of a Richard Nixon bowling orgy at the White House with four Roswell Greys. Drinking Schlitz, talking about Zeta Reticuli, and full insertion. I only caught the footage because I have a Google alert set for "Nixon bowling drunk butthole." I tried sharing it to everyone on Facebook, but I didn't pay the post-boost ransom so only two people saw it.

* * *

"Just make Pop-Tarts twice as goddamn thick," I told the asshole at Kellogg's. I called them weekly to argue about the shittiness of their products, so I could get an occasional coupon I'd never use. "And frost them from edge to edge. I know you have the technology. I read *Wired* magazine." Back in the day, John Harvey Kellogg was fiercely anti-masturbation, so I'm not sure why I even supported their products. Hate the art, not the artist?

* * *

Two guys who flunked out of a trade school for Presbyterian goat herders started an anonymous podcast where they talked about the need for more lax food handling laws, like how more people dying from eating gas station nachos would be a good thing. Each episode began with a cold open of vomiting sounds before the theme music, and was sponsored by MeUndies and a local car wash. The USDA eventually tracked them down because they were using a cracked copy of Adobe Audition that was originally licensed to the trade school. There was an extrajudicial execution two weeks later, which was supposed to be televised, but ironically all video footage got destroyed by a crash of the Adobe Media Encoder program, and nobody had backups.

Dubai and the Taco Bell Day Spa Quest

Not sure how I ended up in Dubai, but I spent hours walking in 117-degree heat trying to find a mythical Taco Bell day spa, where instead of hot stone treatments, they poured scalding nacho cheese on your back and packed your body in smashed-up tortilla chips. The salt is supposed to be exfoliating, I guess. They probably got the chip crumbs from the daily crumbled-up waste at the bottom of the bins, or off the floor. Hot sauce is extra, though.

After three days and nights of no luck with this endless quest, I headed to the airport to ditch my rental car and catch the giant aluminum germ tube for a twenty-hour flight back home. There's absolutely nothing to do in Dubai for free, and I didn't want to get my picture taken on the back of a camel for $800, even if it came with a free t-shirt. In the parking lot with twenty minutes to kill until I could check in, I ate an entire Häagen-Dazs ice cream cake, thinking about the implications of a six-dimensional universe rendered in three dimensions for broadcast television. This makes more sense if you've edited down 360-degree video to straight-up 1080p, but I'm not expecting anyone to follow me here.

Every woman in the airport had long hair on the sides with the top of their scalp shaved in a grid pattern, like some kind of high-fashion, early-90s cyberpunk thing mixed with a male-pattern baldness heavy metal groove. Cast-iron skullet. It could have been a throwback to when Cyndi Lauper used to do the cross-hatching pineapple-looking thing on the sides, but now it was shifted to the upper scalp for some reason. Or maybe Amanda Palmer had a clipper accident, decided to own it, lit Tumblr on fire with pictures of the mangled 'do, something something, profit. I don't know how these things get started; I've worn the same Target jeans and t-shirts for decades. Fashion trends are cyclical and viral, and getting together a bunch of upper-class jet-setters in a single airport terminal proved this more than any laboratory experiment ever could. Even with their weird Trent Reznor hairdos, they were still hot as hell, solid LA 10s with the best breasts money could buy and yoga asses you could never believe. It made me want to hunt for one of those lactation station booths and use it as an impromptu jerk-off station, knock one out before my flight.

"THIS IS A NON-SMOKING TERMINAL. MANY BAGS LOOK ALIKE. IF YOU SEE SOMETHING, SAY SOMETHING. GOD IS GREAT. ALL HAIL JESUS. LOWERING CORPORATE TAXES FOR AIRLINES HELPS US ALL. DO NOT PARK IN THE RED ZONE. YOU WILL BE ASSIMILATED. WE GOT THE FUNK. ONLY HOPE CAN KEEP ME TOGETHER. NINETY-SEVEN OCTANE FUEL IS REQUIRED. STAY BEHIND

THE YELLOW LINE AT ALL TIMES. STANDING FOR THE NATIONAL ANTHEM IS NOW MANDATORY. BLUE LIVES MATTER. THIS IS A NON-SMOKING TERMINAL..."

The announcement played twice every five minutes, reminding me I was still in the purgatory of the terminal. Even with the earbuds blasting an old Indestroy album at top volume (technically their only album, 1987's LP of the same name as the band — the one with "Dead Girls (Don't Say No)" on it), I heard the robotic Moviefone announcer voice of the recording, alternating with pages for people who were lost and probably dead. Sorry, family of Lock Chow Party of Five, they left the Sterile Area, walked out the wrong door and into the spinning turbine of a 737 engine, bloody shredded flesh ejected from the back of the Emirates Airlines plane like confetti shot out of a cannon. Please contact an agent at the service desk to file a luggage claim for their belongings and remains. And remember, all body parts and corpses MUST be checked with a gate agent for an additional twenty-five dollar fee.

Spent most of the flight reading a book about a whale hunter who had a crisis of conscience, decided to start a Tibetan crossbow school in rural Alaska, and died of chronic scoliosis while building log cabins with no modern tools. I think it was a popular blog that got self-published into a book, not sure how I found out about it. Not much plot, but people get too uptight about lack of plot these days, like it's a bad thing. Life has no plot. Nothing has plot, get used to it.

Back home, two dozen hours later, I felt like I couldn't turn my neck anymore without intense pain. Even after being awake for three days straight, I couldn't sleep — too many complimentary Diet Cokes in my system from the long flight. I went to the mall and put fifty dollars in a massage chair, sat around and watched the mall walkers and Sbarro pizza employees. The chair buzzed and vibrated like an old Yugo with snow tires and bad shocks, exactly what I needed. Everyone in the bank of chairs was an old man, and it felt both demeaning and bonding to be there with them. I thought about pitching a reality TV show where old men competitively sat in massage chairs, but I couldn't figure out how to structure the competition, and my only reality TV connection left the business to join ISIS a few years ago. (He thought it was a more positive contribution to society. He was also really into guns and beards. I think he's been droned since then, though. Went to the wrong wedding, if you know what I mean.) Also, you pretty much need T&A to get any reality show off the ground these days.

I heard some kids at the Cinnabon talking about mini-bikes while they shoveled pounds of frosting into their maws. They were trying to find a way to amp up a $300 trail bike from Wal-Mart, the kind with a 100cc gas engine that lasts maybe a month before seizing. They obviously didn't have a stoner buddy who majored in shop class to show them how it's done. I had a friend in high school who tore the similarly sized engine out of a cheap go-kart and put in a beat-up 40-horsepower tractor motor he got at a junkyard. I drove it once and it was beyond scary, like diving out of a plane with no chute scary. It had no windshield, no seatbelt, no protection whatsoever. And it was so goddamn back-heavy, barely touching the gas pedal would pull the front wheels off the ground. The brakes were totally useless, and you can't steer if the wheels aren't touching. I did one lap around his car-strewn yard and it's the closest I've ever been to death.

Can't remember that go-kart dude's name, and I wonder if he's still alive. He was an excellent machinist, probably ended up turning out full-auto AR-15 receivers and got David Koreshed by the ATF. When I knew him, he always had a dozen project cars in his yard, three-hundred dollar clunkers he'd buy and hot-rod or demo derby. Maybe the county got down on him for having too many unregistered vehicles. I'd never know; his last name was Yoder, and so was half my graduating class. Lots of Mennonites in that area.

My power chair must have clicked off after my money ran out, but I completely blacked out and didn't notice it. Went into a weird dream about meeting George Romero at a gang bang and listening to him talk about the Pittsburgh Steelers for an hour. I woke up in the empty mall three hours after closing and thought I was in the zombie apoca-lypse. I ran to find the sporting goods store with guns, but the closest thing I could find was a Victoria's Secret. This happens to me far more often than you'd think.

The Frank Herbert Toilet Amputation

"He was reading *Dune* on the toilet and got so into it, he forgot to move for days, and they ended up amputating his legs because all the nerves were dead. The paramedics had to break down his front door, pry the toilet off the seal on the floor and break it free from his ass at the hospital with a surgical hammer and chisel. He had to pay an orthopedic surgeon five thousand dollars an hour to smash that throne into pieces and extricate his gluteus max, plus the surgical tools were sterile and they charged another ten grand for them. And that's not counting the nurses, anesthesia, supplies, and so on. Total nightmare. I would have broken loose that thing for twenty bucks, and that includes shutting off the water first. Maybe I should invent an emergency toilet breaking tool, sell it on QVC to old people who worry too much about dying on the throne. Million-dollar idea."

RIP in Peace, Cocaine Rod

After an hour of driving through empty streets at night, I found a giant 24-hour warehouse store. Most of them are 24-hour now I guess, especially in the central part of the country, giant aircraft hangars full of furniture, farm clothing, cheap electronics, and frozen chili dogs. After miles and miles of dead coal mining town, there it was: a two-million square foot prefabricated big box of a building, surrounded by 340 acres of parking, all brightly lit like the surface of Mercury. Not a goddamn car in sight.

Right after I navigated through the airlock doors and grabbed a cart, a bored third-shift worker lit up the PA, announced that they were closing liquor sales in five minutes, so rush over to the hundred-yard aisle of death and stock up, you won't be able to for another four hours. I'd been on the wagon for months, but this was the kind of place that makes you want to get loaded, the misery and desolation of the midwestern sprawl, beaten and fucked by decades of the downward spiral.

I shuffled down the gauntlet of booze, looking at all the various industrial-sized bottles and jugs of rotgut. This was the era of value-engineered prepackaged cocktails. Instead of simple bottles of pure rum, gin, vodka, and so on, the aisle was filled with spiked ice teas, "adult" root beers, and premixed cocktails or sodas or mixers fortified with cheap, industrial-grade alcohol. Drinking a thousand calories an hour was practically enforced by law in these parts. I didn't want to buy any alcohol, but I felt like I needed to buy some alcohol.

(Jimmy Carter explained the "spiked" drink phenomenon to me once when we were both at a Jethro Tull concert. His brother was in the booze business — remember Billy Beer? Anyway, under the wrath of George HW, the government raised the excise tax on wine by ninety cents a gallon in 1991, and the adult beverage industry reacted by engineering wine coolers made from malt barley, and inventing products like Zima to cater to underaged drinkers.)

I originally came to the store because I forgot my alarm clock on the trip. I needed to wake up in four hours to go to the funeral of this old college buddy. Well, not really a buddy. It was complicated, and I felt sorry for him, or at least sorry enough to drive halfway across the country and stare at his corpse in the lowest-model wooden box available, probably something sold at this same warehouse store. The motel didn't have a clock/radio — it didn't even have frames on the beds — and my phone was not loud enough to wake me from the full-on Ambien/Tylenol PM one-two knockout I'd be getting into shortly. This wasn't the tier of lodging facility that offered wake-up calls; they barely offered sheets on the bed.

I remembered this article saying the first alarm clocks involved ancient hunters or warriors drinking a bunch of water before they slept. That got me to the beverage aisle of the store. There was a "pop" section, and then a "new age drinks" section, right before the alcohol. I knew I wouldn't make it to the register in seven minutes with any high-test alcohol, and I'm sure that would interact with the armada of sleep medication I'd need after twelve hours in a rented Hyundai economy car with no radio. I found a bunch of bottles of Clearly Canadian, which I was pretty sure had been off the market for a dozen years, so either it was a throwback or it was toxic. I also got a tiny Indiglo travel alarm clock, which I hoped would wake me up.

The funeral was for a guy named Cocaine Rod, who last I heard was convinced the Air Force and/or his parents put microchip implants in his balls, and that's why he couldn't get it up anymore. It had nothing to do with the five grams of cocaine he snorted or smoked every day, of course. He made his living holding fake 5K charity runs all over the Midwest. I don't entirely know the angle; I guess he would take the entry money through the mail, but not get the permits or file for the street closures or whatever you need to do to run a marathon in the city, so a bunch of soccer moms would show up and run through live traffic, but he'd be long gone by then. Maybe he would print up t-shirts, but otherwise it was just an unsupervised death march.

When I first met Cocaine Rod in college, he was running a long con on the resident housing department and his parents, cancelled his lease after making copies of his uncopyable keys through a coke buddy who was an illegal locksmith, and then somehow got a refund of his room and board each month after his parents paid it. He mostly couchsurfed, but hung out at the dorm constantly to shower, use the computers, score coke, and harass freshman girls about how he won the lottery and loved to eat pussy.

Cocaine Rod started out as a business major, but switched about ten minutes into his first semester, when he realized there was no way he could deal with the A-core requirements of calculus, accounting, and macroeconomics plus consume as much cocaine as possible. He vacillated between being majoring in philosophy and something random, depending on the week. Like once he came to my room, offered to split a rock, and then spent an hour talking about how he wanted to be the first cocaine meteorologist. Maybe a good idea for a movie script, but I couldn't see it as a career choice. And I didn't dare touch any drug of his. I knew the mafia would eventually kill him, and I didn't want to accidentally snort some pure rat poison when they tried to hot-shot him.

After a year or two, Cocaine Rod vanished from campus, the parental dole bled dry. Every few months, he'd send me an all-caps email explaining his whereabouts and typically asking me a stupid computer question, like how to scan a picture without a scanner. Once he told me he lived in Nebraska, had a job as a plumber's assistant maintaining blood drain pipes in slaughterhouses, and was marrying a lesbian proctologist so she could get a green card in exchange for colon cancer screenings. Two years later, he was in clown school in Florida, and running a telemarketing scheme selling obsolete Packard Bell laptops to senior citizens.

Once Facebook happened, I'd get a new friend request from Cocaine Rod every few months. He'd drop his phone in the toilet or lose it at a gang-bang, and when he got a replacement, he wouldn't realize you could just log into the same account from the new phone, so he'd create another. He never actually updated about his life, just endless statuses from an online poker game, reposts of porn star pictures, and the occasional "LOL" reply to something I posted. Then a bit of radio silence, and his sister posted from his account, inviting everyone to the funeral, but not saying what happened.

He had some unspecified disease, or maybe he just ate garbage for fifty years and his guts exploded. It's now impossible to find out how people die, since everyone hides everything online, and nobody at the event would say anything except that he was "with God" and the plasticized corpse in the coffin that looked like a third-grader's papier-mâché project "looked good." He ended up having a funeral that was like the opposite of an Indian wedding, because he was way too into George Harrison or something. Like there was a little horse, a trampoline, a lot of people in saris. I think it was an arranged funeral, like his parents picked someone for him to be buried alive with.

His dad looked like an aging Civil War general, and couldn't remember his own son's name half the time. His local friends were all coal miners and juvenile delinquents, who told eulogy after eulogy about getting fucked up and destroying property, which was funny the first five times, but got boring the next fifty. It reminded me of an endless Alcoholics Anonymous meeting with no amends or recovery. And the corpse was so badly embalmed, I wondered if they got it done at an Aldi's grocery store. He resembled an old GI Joe doll that had been left in the yard too long. He even had the same patchy, glue-on fuzz beard and hair.

The catering was decent, but not the kind of stuff you want to eat right before you drive home for 20 hours straight. I wolfed down about twenty microwaved samosas and a chunk of red velvet cake as big as my head, and didn't even make it to the first rest stop on the Ohio Turnpike before disaster struck. RIP in Peace, Cocaine Rod.

Echter Geschmack Ganz Gross!

There was a new place to eat by the mall, a local version of the German version of Kentucky Fried Chicken. The menu isn't really that different, apart from being bilingual. I think they did it to get around a trademark dispute or franchise agreement stipulation. I rode my bike there and got a bucket of hot wings, which weren't bad, but a crucial error because I needed to finish reading a computer science textbook I was studying, and I got grease all over the pages. The damn book cost $600 new, and I'd never be able to sell it back.

Couldn't get the lock on my bike undone, so I left it chained to the side of the building and walked across town to a music store that only sold harmonicas and tambourines. The owner looked like that Blues Traveler singer, and wore a full-length sword on his belt, which kept knocking stuff over as he waddled around the house. "Tiny houses are just single-wide trailers for hipster idiots," he told me, while I looked at a signature Ozzy Osborne harmonica from Hohner. (Model M666) "I grew up in a trailer park, and you don't see me getting my own show on HGTV."

I thought about completely ripping off the guy's life and making it into a reality TV show, like a mix of *Pawn Stars* and maybe *Hoarders*. But I was sure this was a lawsuit waiting to happen, especially if I actually made any money on it. I put back the Ozzy harp — couldn't tell if it was previously used, and the cross on it wasn't upside-down — and walked to the Army-Navy store, hoping I could buy enough freeze-dried food to spend the next year hidden in my apartment, so I didn't have to talk to anyone ever again.

Ceiling Fan Lickers and Horse People on Subways

I kept seeing an ad in the back of the free paper for a guy who would come to your house and lick your ceiling fans from stem to stern. I wasn't sure if you were supposed to pay him, or if he paid you; no prices or fees were mentioned on the ad or his web site. Maybe this is illegal. Maybe it's a sting. Either way, I'm not sure I'd feel comfortable having a guy who licked ceiling fans hang around my house. I'm sure his breath would be horrible. And what happens after he's done? Does he want you to jerk him off, or does he sit there talking about sports? Is he a Yankees or Mets fan? What happens when you run into him a month later at the Container Store in the mall? Do you say hi? It's an awkward situation. But he ran that damn ad every week. He must have been getting some traction from it.

One time I met a woman from the personals in the back of the free paper. It didn't work out, and then I constantly ran into her in the subway. She was always trying to ride her horse onto the train. I don't know if that's technically legal or not, or if the horse needs a second subway pass, although I'm sure you can get some bullshit piece of paper saying it's an assistance animal or emotional support horse or whatever. If Winston Churchill was getting prescriptions to say he could legally plow through endless bottles of Johnnie Walker Red every day in prohibition-era America, I'm sure some asshole podiatrist can write you a slip for your seeing-eye pony for fifty bucks.

Anyway, she would get the horse up the stairs — this was in Queens, where all the subways are elevated — and then trot back and forth on the platform, trying to avoid the MTA cops. I didn't know her plan on the other end; if she got into the city, she would have to lead the animal up the stairs to the surface, and then back down again to return, and can horses even walk up stairs? I thought when they put a horse in that dude's office in *Animal House*, they had to cut it in half to get it back down? I might be thinking of a different movie.

The horse lady looked like a horse person. I don't mean she looked like a horse; I mean she looked like the kind of person who would own a horse, spend their weekends on grooming, saddle adjusting, dressage, and whatever the hell you do when you have an equine animal. It's like when you can look at a PTA mom and say, "I know she was a cheerleader when she was in school, and is going to try to pay with an expired coupon." It made perfect sense.

Horses honestly bother me. My worst nightmare is staying at an exclusive waterfront resort where they have sunset horse rides on the beach, because that basically means if you go on long walks in your bare feet on the white sands of the exotic island, you're walking in loads of horse shit. You're catching anthrax or the bubonic plague or whatever is in horse manure. I only stay in horse-free hotels, as a general rule of thumb. I didn't want to get kicked in the head by a pony, or catch a loose shoe to the face, or become a trampling victim. Didn't horses start that big fire in Chicago, or was that a cow? Same difference. Fuck everything barnyard-related, except Wrangler jeans, because they have the U-shaped crotch, for comfort.

Larry King Lives

Freddy got a video editing job with CNN, a contract gig where he had to carefully edit all 6,120 episodes of *Larry King Live* and change the titles and graphics to *Larry King Lives*, because Larry King had just been assassinated a few months before, and they couldn't imply he was alive in the title without getting sued for slander or libel or something. "I'm only like a year in. It takes me at least two or three hours per 60-minute episode. I don't even know why the fuck they need these in the archives, but they pay me per episode. I can listen to like six or seven brutal Satanic death metal albums per job."

I was trying to calculate how much Fruit by the Foot I could eat before my entire circulatory system turned into high-fructose corn syrup. I think it's 1.2 ounces of blood per pound, and I'm pushing 200, so that's 240 ounces; a six-pack of FbtF is 4.5 ounces. So that's just shy of 54 boxes. But I don't know how efficient the kidneys or liver or whatever are, like at stripping that stuff out of your digestive system. I bet you'd have to eat a few hundred boxes and pace yourself to get it to work. You could probably blend them and inject it intravenously, but that would probably kill you. Well, so would eating a hundred boxes of pure sugar with a little bit of fruit flavoring. I'm not sure why I started doing this. I think it was related to watching that liquid breathing thing in *The Abyss*.

"Man, you would not believe Larry King's slow descent into madness over the years," he said. "I mean, the guy is cool as fuck, but watching hundreds of episodes of anybody except maybe Dick Clark is a testament to our mortality. It's like one of those fast-motion timescape videos of fruit rotting. What was that fuckin' Russian film that was all time-lapse stuff like that? The one with the John Cage music."

"It was Philip Glass. I can't remember the name, except it was something impossible, like *Koyyyawahaiaannbanna-naramaannaisisqqattriscitsksi*." I actually used to work in the same building as Glass's recording studio, not that I knew what he looked like. I think I saw some big concert of his at MoMA but I can't remember one measure of the music. Something about Egyptians I think. "I have it on DVD somewhere, but every time I start watching it, I fall asleep. I can't see how you can edit video all day like that."

"Fucking unholy Satanic metal, my friend. Kill god, shit on the altar. It's what keeps me warm at night."

The Failure Cascade

A Jersey City paralegal with an insufferable crush on Rob Lowe emailed me at work, ten or fifteen messages an hour, in all caps. This had been going on for at least a month. She found my barbed-wire fence collection on an abandoned Geocities page, and felt a great need to tell me how she had a barbed wire tattoo on her ankle and wanted to get laid on a cruise ship during a water emergency. I already knew this was going to fail spectacularly, but I couldn't ignore it or walk away.

The cruise ship thing seemed relevant because I knew someone who used to work for Holland America in Seattle, or maybe she worked for the company that built the ships for Holland America — all I remember is she took a lot of free trips, but always ended up with listeria or MRSA or some death plague that involved eating hundreds of Cipro tablets for a month or two. Maybe there's something enticing to some women about having sex on a sinking ship which is also drenched in flesh-eating bacteria, black mold, and everything short of airborne AIDS. After anonymous sex and barebacking with strangers on video got boring, maritime-based disaster sex was the next logical step.

(I don't collect barbed wire, by the way. Well, I did for like a week in 1997. I think I saw it on a TV show, or found a very persuasive LiveJournal about it, made me think it would be something I could do in my spare time. Was there LiveJournal back in 1997? Actually, it could have been because of Pamela Anderson's arm tattoo, and that horrible action-adventure movie of the same name she made back then. After a few days of trying to bid on pieces of fencing on eBay, I lost interest. But I'd written about 50,000 words on the hobby, stretched across a few hundred pages in a web site, and didn't feel like deleting it, so it sat to rot. Maybe there's a reason to keep old web pages going, but what do I know. Nobody reads my web pages. Nobody reads anything longer than five words anymore. Nobody's reading this.)

Normally, I ignore these emails, but work was boring, and she sent pictures last week. They were unbelievably good, like bathing suit model good. I was probably being catfished, but I had nothing better going on. In my response to that day's usual torrent of mails, I said I liked the pictures, but didn't know how to swim and said I couldn't meet her for drinks because I was temporarily living in an isolation tank with a bad case of the bubble boy disease. I thought playing hard-to-get was the angle there, especially because I didn't have the money to impress anyone in this town. I thought maybe if I could keep things going, I might enjoy the back-and-forth, get a few more good pictures out of the deal. The chase is better than the catch. Motörhead songs are rarely incorrect, but Lemmy also wrote that Ozzy song "Mama I'm Coming Home," so I could be wrong here.

It was Friday, so after work, I hiked to the local C-Town grocery to get a rotisserie chicken, a bulk thing of crackers, and sixteen cans of aerosol cheese. I needed supplies to make it through the weekend; I planned on writing an adventure game like Zork, but about the Andrei Chikatilo killings. I didn't tell New Jersey any of that — copyright fears, and not everybody is into serial killers who sexually assaulted, murdered, and mutilated at least fifty-two women and children between 1978 and 1990. I'd probably stay up until six in the morning HTML-izing a bunch of translations of Russian psychiatric evaluations, go partially insane, and write her a twisted dispatch that put all the cards on the table and forever fuck any chance I'd have at getting a picture of her tits. I'm not a very good strategist, and my dating life would have been much better if I installed that parental control software and locked my email access after sundown.

* * *

I feel like I've written this same story a dozen times: "Jon rides the subway home, spends an entire weekend in isolation, trying to get laid online and/or find some meaning in life by pursuing a hopeless hobby." And honestly, this basically happened every week for like five years of my time in New York. I remember FreshDirect expanding into Queens right around the time *Grand Theft Auto: Vice City* came out on the Playstation 2, and I would go home at 5:00 on Friday night and play *GTA* until early in the morning on Monday, eating whatever garbage I could get delivered to my door. I was supposed to be writing my third book, or maybe living the life of a functional adult in their early thirties, but I didn't know what to write or how to be a normal human being.

And when I write any of the stories like the ones in this book, whatever you call them — microfiction or flash or gonzo fiction or whatever — the more of these I do, the more I realize I'm writing the same five or six stories over and over again. I think ten years ago, when I started thinking about the possibility of stealing Hunter Thompson's gonzo journalism shtick and using it for fiction, it made total sense. Instead of writing autobiographical fiction or creative nonfiction and lamenting that I couldn't write "weird" stuff, I'd use a first-person participatory story, and wrap it around a core piece of some observational opinion piece. Instead of writing about how Richard Nixon was a weirdo or publishing excruciating reviews of old Dokken records, I'd write a story about how I used to hang out with Richard Nixon and listen to Dokken records with him. And that worked, until it didn't.

I got into the whole gonzo thing because I originally started writing this completely exhausting first-person fiction. My first book was a completely unreadable dense chunk of wood that according to one reviewer, "was nothing more than a list of every place the author ate lunch in 1992." I had a couple of good stories in me from this era, but ultimately any autobiographical creative nonfiction (or whatever it's called this week) is less about how good the story is, and more about how much the reader identifies with the writer, or wants to be them, or whatever. And I think I started writing because the popularity contest of high school was an abject failure for me. I am not a person that people like. I've known that for almost forty years. If I'd known the world of self-publishing was all about developing your own cult of personality, I honestly would have started collecting stamps instead.

And I get it, "write what you want to write, even if nobody else will read it," etc. But at this point, I've strip-mined my past so much, and I have nothing I want to write about, so I keep writing about the same six things. Every one of these books has a scene where me and Fat Mike go to a 7-Eleven. Every one has a scene where I'm in an airport waiting for a plane, or listening to an old man scream obscenities at a cashier. I'm out of ideas, and I'm stuck in my house until further notice, so I have nothing left to write about.

This is probably why people only write murder mysteries and romance novels. They come up with the one-sentence summary of the book, then write the book. Why read the whole book if you can read the summary? I guess that's why there's an entire culture built upon big twists and surprise endings and people who get pissed off about spoilers. I know I've already bitched about this too much either.

I never do this, the meticulous planning and pitching and plotting on index cards. I always write just to write, and then later try to make it into a book, which is probably why this entire book is 99% done and I haven't even titled it yet. I've already created this complicated failure cascade where I hate the book before it's done, but it's mid-December and it has to be out by the end of the year, so I need to rush this goddamn thing, even though I know nobody will read it, because it doesn't have a catchy summary like "it's about a dolphin trainer who loses his wife to lyme disease and learns to love again." This is also why if I had a basement, I'd probably have about $400,000 of model railroad equipment in it and would stop thinking about ever writing again.

Anyway, let's finish the story of me wasting away a weekend doing nothing, which I'm sure I've already written in my last six or eight books. As usual, I'll crash all of Act Three in a single paragraph that does little to help the story. Hold my beer.

* * *

By the time I got home from the grocery store, unpacked my supplies, and speed-ate an entire family-size bag of Doritos, New Jersey wrote me three times, something about how she had a 20-year-old kid (she previously said she was 25, so what the fuck, did she get knocked up in pre-school?) and she was trying to get him into a pornography addiction recovery program, because he quit school, ran up $50,000 in phone tolls on 1-900 numbers (I didn't even know those still existed) and fucked everything in the house. She also sent several thousand words of her *West Wing* slash fiction work-in-progress, a Sam Seaborn/Toby Ziegler romance story with an okay plot ark, but very weak writing, and a few pictures of her old Audi 5000 with the unintended acceleration problem, which I think was supposed to impress me? And she said she suffered from fibromyalgia. It was going to be a long night.

The Reason I Write Too Many Stories about Lawn Equipment Is My Short Tenure as a Lawn and Garden Salesman in 1987-1989

It's sunny outside, and I'm high on sleep medication and Ativan, sitting in my backyard with a broken chainsaw, staring at topographical maps of Sweden printed on high thread-count silk bed sheets. (The Air Force used to give them to U-2 pilots flying over Eastern Europe, so they could walk to freedom if they had to punch out of the plane.) I spent all day reading an article about how the Russians want to open an orbital space station as a casino where you can hire prostitutes and kill them, since international law doesn't exist there, but they don't even have the budget to send food up to their current cosmonauts. Also I think this was maybe in a Dave Barry column, or maybe Mike Royko, so it could have been satire. I would be all for going up in a space station if I could afford it, but I'm sure there's some damn thing that would medically disqualify me, like you couldn't have seasonal allergies, even though you spend the whole trip locked in a hermetically sealed outfit breathing pure oxygen. I don't remember why I have the broken chain saw with me. Aesthetics, I guess.

My neighbor Bro drove his riding lawn mower into his above-ground swimming pool... no idea how he caught enough air to clear the 48-inch high side wall. I heard the landing, but didn't see the takeoff. A ramp must have been involved, but there wasn't one at the scene of the crime. I was surprised he managed to stick the takeoff, and not hit the thin-walled side of that piece of shit pool and spill thousands of gallons of chlorinated water all over his yard, killing the grass for the next year. He's got that kind of bad luck.

Bro suffered from extreme generalized epilepsy, although the family insists it was demonic possession, and forced him to get rectal dilation done every fortnight from an evangelical arborist that goes town to town like an Irish Traveler, performing unnecessary homeopathic procedures on the gullible, sealing driveways, and cutting down dead trees. There are a lot of dead trees in this neighborhood — not sure if it's something in the groundwater, or a disease, some kind of tree AIDS that could be blamed on vegetable morality by the local government. Maybe the traveler causes it, driving poison stakes into trees at night, then coming back a week later to get people to pay him for his arborist skills.

Bro stumbled over to my house, adorned in Judas Priest swim trunks, his upper body sunburned a bright red. Bro's legal first name was actually Broseph, or Bro for short. People can legally do that. Isn't it Sweden or Denmark that makes people pick from a list of like 768 normal-sounding names when they have a kid? Someone should look into that here. We're a few short years from half the fast-food cashiers and dishwashers in this country being named Pokémon.

"Did you see what I just did?" He gestured to the swimming pool with his tallboy can of Red, White, and Blue beer. "Fuckin' Lawn Boy went right in the water. I think I caught some volts off the tractor engine too. The dynamo, or magneto, or whatever the fuck it's called."

"I think it's an alternator and not a dynamo, but I haven't studied the electrical system of your particular riding mower. I don't know if it uses AC or DC current," I said. I wondered if the jolt made his epilepsy worse, or if it magically cured him. "How are you going to get that thing out of your pool?"

He tipped back the can, drank a straight twenty ounces of brew in one pull, then belched. "Fuck if I know. Rent a helicopter maybe. Or drain the pool and disassemble the whole fuckin' thing, but nobody's got time for that. I think the fuckin' tractor is still running. I was blacked out. Damn near drowned. I'm afraid to go back in to shut the fuckin' thing off, get fuckin' shocked again. Fuck!"

"If the engine can't get air, it can't run. Unleaded gasoline isn't thermobaric. It probably sucked pool water straight into the cylinder and choked it out, and now you're going to have to rebuild that engine pronto, before it rusts solid. But good luck fishing it out. Maybe get a crane from the rent-a-center. Or a winch and some ramps, at least."

"Fuck that, I'm not paying for tools. That's un-American. And I'm sure as shit not draining that pool. It took me two weeks to fill that fuckin' thing with a garden hose, and I couldn't take a shower the whole time. I'll get some bleach or system shock to put in there, it should be fine. What the fuck are you doing with those maps, anyway? Are you going to Australia?"

"Um, Sweden."

"Too bad, dude. I know a lot about Australia. I took a bunch of shrooms and went to that new *Mad Max* movie, paid for 3-D and IMAX and the special glasses and everything. It was a god damn religious experience, but I wouldn't want to spend a whole day in a plane to see it in person. Maybe just rent it, or steal a copy from the library."

"Don't worry, I'm not going to Sweden. It's a Tylenol PM thing. I should probably stop taking this stuff every day." I still didn't know why I had the disassembled chain saw. And the more I thought about it, he wasn't going to find a helicopter rental place for less than the cost of his house.

Either he'd need to get ten guys to lift it, or maybe disassemble the damn thing piece by piece. Johnny Cash meme.

Wolfman and Wolverines

A Wolfman Jack-looking dude who looked like he was wearing a Chewbacca mask sucked on a bottle of Rescue Remedy herbal stress juice and talked to a first-grade class in a drug rehab center about how his parents were puppeteers and that somehow caused his rampant huffing addiction. "My daddy had a thirty-string Czech marionette. Hardest ones to handle, because there's no central rod. Lots of controls for the mouth, ears, the whole deal. All hand-carved. Took all his skill to operate that thing every day, so once the seizures started, that's when he turned to glue. Huffing's genetic, you know." None of the kids were listening. Everyone was on the nod, pumped full of enough Sublocade to keep them off hillbilly heroin. They could barely walk — a dozen heavily-tattooed orderlies had to wheel everyone into the community room, watch them to make sure nobody swallowed their tongue. Real *One Flew Over the Cuckoo's Nest* stuff.

During the speech about the puppet master, a battalion of Cuban special forces paratroopers landed in the football field while the orderlies watched, straight out of *Red Dawn*. But instead of opening up their machine guns into the adolescent treatment center, they set up a catering table and started banging out Cuban sandwiches. Food trucks were passé; the latest craze was foodie "experiences," like a high-speed chase in a Mustang like *Bullit*, but that Highland Green '68 Mustang Fastback is towing a taco trailer full of carnitas. The administrator who ran the clinic watched too much Food Network in his downtime, ate at as many Michelin-star restaurants as he could afford and wanted to be hip with the newest trends. Food-wise, the institution kept on top of things; medical-wise, not so much. At least a dozen people a week died because the hospital still did pre-frontal lobotomies and insulin shock therapy.

Wolfman got his fifty bucks, a cold sandwich, and a stamp on his community service card. Only 47,768 hours to go on his parole sentence. He paid a guy to count him on a roadside trash cleaning crew every day, so that was a dozen hours a week. But he did the math, and he'd likely still have tens of thousands of hours left on his tab when he died, even if he ate enough vitamins to live to be a hundred. He called the prison once to ask if they could just lock him back up, credit him 168 hours a week and maybe more for good behavior, but they said he'd have to pay for his incarceration, at a rate of five grand a month, plus expenses.

Wolfman originally got arrested for selling hash on a plane to an undercover federal air marshal. You can legally buy weed in like 37 states now; hell, it's hard to go to Vegas and *not* buy a cannabis product. But it was a federal charge, because they were in the air. Even with weed legal in his state, it would take a national reversal for it to go away. And the bible belt ain't lettin' that happen, not on their watch.

He hauled his gear out to his Chevy Vega and drove to a place that sold real Cuban sandwiches, not the shit the catering company was ladling out to the drugged-up kids. No pickles, of course. Fuck pickles.

THE HATE TANK

"Pizza party!" The M-1 Abrams tank commander stopped his sixty-ton machine of death in front of a local 'za joint so his crew could jump out and fuck some low-quality college town pies. The four-man crew got drunk on cheap draft beer and ate half-raw pizza straight from the oven while shooting their sidearms into the ceiling, killing a dozen people hiding in the attic.

While they chowed down Viking-style with no silverware, a disgruntled construction worker from the hamburger joint next door jumped in the tank, gunned the engine, and took off, smashing cars in his path with the mine plow on the front of the combat vehicle. He must have played enough *Call of Duty* to figure out the controls, because he deftly navigated the 67-ton beast with no problems. The commander thought about going after him, but didn't want to get up from his plate of chicken wings. "Hell, most of our combat losses are friendly fire. This technically improves our stats. Might as well let one go to the universe every now and again, know what I mean?"

They finished their lunch, shot the pizza joint owner in the head, broke open the gumball machine for kicks, then hoofed it to a nearby Lazarus department store, which was offering an additional five percent off all men's department purchases, due to the city siege. They thought about getting new cologne, because spending sixteen days in the close confines of a tank turret without showering can get slightly aromatic. But other than fashion wear and luggage, there wasn't much to be had in the store. They didn't even have an electronics department.

"Buy some scarves. You can't go wrong with cashmere. It's a good gift for a chick you haven't been dating that long. Don't go with any jewelry. Beginner's mistake." A salesman in a shark-skin suit rapped with the tank loader, tried to talk him into buying a few thousand dollars in useless accessories not covered by the siege discount. "I mean, if you really want to wow her, a watch is a good one, but nobody wears watches anymore. I don't even know how to tell time, personally. Hey Siri, is it still Monday?"

Artillery rounds exploded in the parking lot, a group of insurgents across Mall Road with Chinese-made mortars. "Don't worry, those guys can't aim for shit. Remember when you were in trigonometry class in high school, and everyone was like 'when the hell would I ever use this in real life?' Well, now is when you use that shit, and nobody remembers it. This is the problem with an all-child soldier army. You need advanced math. You could do it with a computer, but they've got five-million-dollar tanks that are still using vacuum tubes like it's the Fifties."

[SOH CAH TOA. *Sine = Opposite/Hypotenuse. Cosine = Adjacent/Hypotenuse. Tangent = Opposite/Adjacent. This is use-*

less for external ballistics. You end up with something like
$d=2*V^2/a*cos(a)*sin(a)$, *which doesn't account for air drag, the*
movement of the earth (Coriolis Effect), or the curvature of the
earth. Math is hard!]

An 81-mm mortar, perfectly aimed with an optimum arc, hit right in the middle of the accessories department, the blunt-pointed tip of the finned shell going straight in the left eyeball of the salesman before knocking through his skull and exploding. It looked just like that scene in *Terminator 2*, except his face wasn't made out of liquid metal, and it wasn't hokey computer graphics rendered on a farm of SGI computers that were about as fast as a modern digital watch.

* * *

Speaking of treaded-vehicle mall destruction, International Harvester invented a ten thousand-ton machine that was a combination killdozer and mall recycler. It could run through the walls of a department store and grind down the brick, asbestos, and plaster into a fine dust that could be used to make children's playground surfaces or entomb homeless people in a mass grave. They planned to sell thousands of them to companies destroying old malls in the Midwest to turn them into strip malls that nobody would go to, but that would rake in tax incentives from local governments.

"I've invented the perfect killing machine," said the company president at a press conference in an Arby's at an oasis on the Ohio turnpike. "I don't care what you goddamn tear-jerker pansies say about the death of retail. This machine will fuck you up. DE-MALL THE COUNTRY! WOULD YOU LIKE SOME MAKING FUCK BERZERKER!" He got behind the wheel of the tank, fired off 500 rounds of 7.62mm from the side gun of the war machine, then ran straight through a combination Hardee's/Popeye's chicken, grinding the fast-food restaurant into a greasy cloud of brick powder. (There's a promotional video of this online, somewhere.)

* * *

(Fun fact: Popeye's Famous Fried Chicken founder Al Copeland died of cancer of the salivary glands.)

* * *

I'd spent the first few hours of the war in the mall, ironically enough playing first-person shooter games at the Bally arcade. I probably should have invested more time in getting ready for the apocalypse, but I'm always the last to figure stuff out. I generally don't start packing for a trip until the SuperShuttle is in front of my house laying on the horn. I think I had a few granola bars at home, and I could always shoplift some camping supplies or a thing of waterproof matches so I could start a bonfire or whatever the hell you do during an apocalypse.

"Do we even know who is on what side?" I asked the guy at the hot dog bar while sucking down a chili dog with extra cheese. I generally don't eat hot dogs for a meal, but everything else in the food court wasn't open for lunch yet.

"The belligerents, you mean? I think it's the federal government, the South Korean army, and the rechargeable battery division of Panasonic versus an insurgent group led by a former Junior ROTC group from the local high school, the Army Reserves, a cult with allegiance to North Korea, and a Pinkerton's security team. Lots of non-combatants out there, and a group of Mennonites protesting the whole thing. Some Buddhists were lighting themselves on fire, but I guess that was unrelated."

"Are you guys getting any new video games soon?" I said. "I heard about this new LaserDisc one where you're a ninja and you can split a dude's head open with an axe, and like blood and brains and shit come out."

"Hell, I don't even know if this mall is going to be standing next week. Before this war started, Simon announced they were going to triple the rents. But if you let me know in advance, I can special-order giant two-pound hot dogs."

* * *

I ate so many hot dogs waiting for the McDonald's to open for lunch, thought I was going to shit my pants. There's a certain art to consuming that much cased meat without taking a dump in your jeans while you walk through your day. Acquired skill. I don't know why I ate ten of the questionable links, because I really wanted a Quarter Pounder, but I ended up puking in a mall fountain and going home before the starchy arches even switched over from breakfast. And it wasn't a working fountain, either — they emptied it a decade before, probably because of water leaks. My meaty chunder spread across a dry brick bed filled with spare change and empty Karmelkorn packages.

I don't know when it happened exactly, but I bet at some point, a grad student with too much time on their hands is going to write a paper theorizing that all history should be divided into two eras: before and after you could order a Quarter Pounder without cheese for twenty cents less. At one point, a Quarter Pounder with cheese was an option, an upcharge. But after some crossover point, maybe in the mid-90s, the Quarter Pounder with cheese was the standard, and the stock Quarter Pounder vanished from the menu. Sure, you could order a Quarter Pounder and hold the cheese, but it cost the same price. Probably had to do with Greenpeace. Or maybe the Arch Deluxe silently killed that option, so they could put that and the McPizza and the McSpaghetti and McShit Sandwich and everything else on the menu and still fit it on one page.

The mortar fire stopped, I think. The insurgents made it across Mall Road, then took a right, heading south and following the A bus line, towards the Rax Roast Beef restaurant. They'd avoid the mall itself, waiting until they could regroup and concentrate fire on the Target back-to-school specials starting next Thursday. I managed to get home, change my pants, and live to see another day.

Post-dialectic Discourse in the Works of GG Allin and Alanis Morissette

I signed up for the legal aid thing at work, so I could draw up a will. I met with a paralegal over the phone and tried to explain to her that I wanted a funeral like GG Allin's, where everyone got to piss on my corpse while it was in the open casket. She said that wasn't legally possible because of health codes, and hung up on me.

* * *

One of the main reasons I never got into amputee porn was the fear that I would get 100% all-in on it, then accidentally step on a landmine or get a gangrenous toenail and lose a leg, and then everyone would say, "isn't it ironic?" and I would get the Alanis Morissette song stuck in my head and blow someone in a theater.

* * *

The Failure Cascade

Started writing a negative Yelp review about that A&W hot dog stand in the Netherlands that amputated my left hand because I tried to pay with a Discover card, then I realized that was probably a dream. Nobody takes the Discover card anymore.

Hot Karl's Goodbye and the Taliban Bugzilla Database

There was a work party that night, a wild banger that promised to unfold into an international criminal conspiracy, and the drinks were supposed to be free, so it was heavily attended. An old-timer in QA named Karl who had been around since the DOS 3.30 days was trying to get fired so he could cash out his 401K early with no tax penalty (I don't think that actually works) and arranged an unofficial all-company fiesta to celebrate the birthday of Benito Mussolini. He used his company Amex to buy like ten cases of Everclear and every pre-made sandwich from the local D'Agostino's grocery store, then filled a kiddie pool with institutional-size cans of spaghetti, even though Mussolini banned spaghetti. (He also bought a deli tray with just meat and cheese, and no vegetarian options. That was a fireable offense, but his receipt from D'Agostino's just said "DELI" on it, so they couldn't blame him for it without further documentation. And someone threw the entire tray out the window, so there was no proof.)

Just to get people started, Karl told everyone you could drink Everclear if you were on Atkins, because it has no sugar in it, and that's bullshit because drinking any alcohol stops ketosis, but what the fuck do I know, because I'm a fat bastard and I'm always bitching about how Atkins doesn't work and they're all going to die of heart attacks. (Spoiler alert: ten years later, two of them did die of heart attacks, and none of them kept the weight off. Another one died of a knitting-related accident, but this was allegedly unrelated. He was knitting a scarf to wear while eating pound after pound of greasy bacon, so I'm going to say it was related.)

Karl wasn't exactly svelte, and he also had a sort of Krusty the clown thing going with his hair, although it was gray instead of blue. His skin was the same color of yellow though, probably hepatitis or some other liver ailment. I think he had a couple of teenage kids who never talked to him anymore, and a strange fixation with going to Cambodia or Vietnam or something to get an arranged marriage. Everyone called him Hot Karl behind his back. The VP of Engineering always called him Karl Junior straight to his face, which they both found hilarious.

Anyway, annoying sales and marketing people got blackout drunk on 95% pure grain alcohol and started punching holes in the walls and throwing furniture out of windows. (How were they even opening the windows? This was one of those floor-to-ceiling glass buildings, totally sealed shut. Maybe someone had a glass cutter, or fucked someone in facilities who had a special key.) Most of the suits didn't know or acknowledge Hot Karl whatsoever. There was no food of any substance left after that deli tray got tossed. The sandwiches were all garbage, and the couple of decent roast beef ones vanished immediately. Karl called a Cambodian place and tried to order more food, but they brought over five cases of landmines and a gallon of agent orange.

I drank maybe a dozen shots of Everclear and ate a bag of stale Doritos I kept hidden in my laptop bag for emergency purposes before I wised up and left the party. Caught a subway home, stopped at the K-Mart store at Astor Place and bought sixteen games for the XBox, and I don't even have an XBox. I apparently opened all of the games while standing on the platform waiting for the train, ensuring that I could not return them, and then threw them onto the tracks so the third rail would hopefully spark across the aluminum discs and make them explode or possibly derail the train straight into me so I wouldn't have to go to work hungover the next day. (It didn't work.)

I caught a train with no air conditioning, sat down and fell asleep from the groggy heat, but woke in a panic a half-hour later and realized I was one stop away from home. I do this all the time. The extreme jolt of fight-or-flight adrenaline is the closest I can afford to crack cocaine, so maybe I'm doing it on purpose. Because of the panic adrenaline, and also because I threw up back in the K-Mart all over a life-sized figurine of Kathy Ireland in the women's fashions section, I was 100% sober by the time I got out of the subway.

During the train blackout, I had a vivid dream that I was riding a series of local subways and trolleys from Los Angeles to Elkhart, Indiana. I was with jazz fusion bassist Jeff Berlin, who bet me twenty dollars he could teach me the entire Rush song "2112" before we got to Indiana. This was a sucker's bet, because the series of 167 interconnecting train rides and the ensuing transfers and layovers would take us months. Plus, it's a twenty-minute song, but at least five minutes is intros and outros and that part in the middle where Alex Lifeson dicks around with tuning up the acoustic guitar, so it's really just fifteen minutes of bass.

Anyway, Berlin gave me an esoteric method of memorizing the notes in order that had to do with smelling the colors of the tones, which made total sense in the dream, but I could not comprehend this at all mentally when I woke up. We were both playing these matching Strawberry Shortcake bass guitars, a cheap Chinese clone of a Fender made out of plywood and plastic, but they did play very well, with amazingly low action and no fret buzz. They were also scratch-and sniff or impregnated with some artificial scent, because my bass was modeled after the character Blueberry Muffin and smelled strongly of artificial berry odor. But I somehow lost the practice bass on the train, left it in the bar car or something.

I also realized, while we were learning the "Grand Finale" part of the song, that the last section of the South Shore Line interurban railroad going east from Chicago would dump me off at the airport in South Bend, Indiana, and there wasn't another train going to Elkhart from there, because the locals didn't believe in public transit. And there wasn't Uber, because everyone drove pickup trucks. I was also starving, and I guessed correctly that there would be nothing to eat at the airport, unless I left security and walked five miles to a Taco Bell.

I gave up and decided to just fly back to LA, pay full-price for a ticket with no warning. But I'd been flagged by the TSA for Secondary Security Screening Selection, where an "SSSS" is always printed on your boarding pass (buy enough last-minute tickets and this will happen to you, too), and every time you fly when flagged SSSS, you get pulled aside and end up going to second base with a TSA agent, having all your luggage scrutinized, and usually miss your flight. This airport was smaller than the apartment I had in college that I rented for $177 a month, had one metal detector, and when the quad-S came up, the TSA dude freaked the fuck out like if Osama bin Ladin himself showed up at the airport and presented valid picture ID. He dragged me into the back of an abandoned Cinnabon and was ready to beat the shit out of me until he got a manager on the phone who told him to stand the fuck down and just give me the full-court press and see if I was hiding a grenade under my balls.

Eighteen hours later, I arrived at LAX, and every restaurant in the concourse was under construction or missing. (The missing ones had "footage missing" signs on them, a nod to Hollywood test screenings, I guess.) I asked a gate agent about it, and she got on the intercom and started screaming, "WE'RE GETTING A SHAKE SHACK, SHUT THE FUCK UP SIR." Luckily that In-n-Out on Sepulveda is open until 1:30 on Fridays and Saturdays, so I could walk the 1.7 miles in about a half an hour, provided I didn't get hit by a car.

Anyway, Hot Karl the QA guy didn't get fired, as he hoped. Someone on the North side of middle-manager hell got him a promotion, and they sent him to rural Pakistan to start up a new lab with local talent, each new hire making a million Pakistani rupees a year. (Sounds great, but that's like six grand in US dollars. I guess you can rent a house for like $40 a month, but whatever.) Didn't make it more than a few months before he got upset he wouldn't get a Cambodian wife, decided to join the Taliban, and became their Director of Quality Assurance. He ran their Bugzilla bug tracking database out of a cave in the mountains. (Yes, of course the Taliban uses Bugzilla. I think they helped design it.) He'd eventually die of chronic gout, which I didn't even know was possible. No idea if he ever cracked open that 401K, or what the tax implications are for being an enemy combatant.

Raw Power

"BLOOD OF CHRIST!" Grandpa Jones kept scratching at the lottery tickets, trying to win the free trip to Hawaii, even though he'd never been more than ten miles from town, and he absolutely would not fly, because he thought airplanes were a communist plot. "NONE OF THESE HAVE THE RIGHT NUMBERS! THIS IS RIGGED BY DEMOCRATS AND COMMUNISTS" He took off his belt with his silver-stained hands, wrapped it around his neck, and searched the apartment for a place he could tie off the other end and choke himself to death.

* * *

Someone told me you could kill bedbugs by listening to the third Stooges album at top volume, but you had to find the pressing with the original 1973 mix that Iggy did, not the bullshit David Bowie mix that is on most copies. I knew I'd end up with an entire shelf of various versions of *Raw Power*, and still have an extreme parasite infestation. When I eventually got the right copy (it's the 1997 "legacy edition" mix on CD), it blew out my amp within fifteen seconds.

* * *

A county road crew buried the body of a dead teenaged hooker in a pothole near my house. They cased her body in asphalt like she was Han Solo. The only reason they got caught is the local news channel sent out a camera crew to investigate, because it was so unusual that the county would fix any of the roads. And then when the News 7 Action Team got there, the corpse was totally visible, because the crew did such a piss-poor job with the repair.

If You Want Blood (You Got It)

My boss's wedding had a Mad Dog 20/20 fountain and raw vegan hot dogs with no buns. I know you can, like, legally eat raw hot dogs — they cook them in the factory — but that shit is disgusting. Also, these ones looked like maybe they'd spent a bit too much time out of the fridge. I don't like to go to weddings, and I don't like this boss, a save-the-whales blowhard who once told me he found canned vegan ham "enticing," but someone said there would be booze and free food. They were only technically right.

I talked to the best man, and in between bong hits, he told me the over/under on the marriage was three months. He sent me the URL to an online gambling site to put money on it, but it was a .ru domain, and when I went to it through the Tor browser to sneak a peek, it launched a million pop-ups, and didn't use HTTPS. No thanks. I might as well run an ad during the Super Bowl with my credit card number on it.

Walked to a VA clinic next door to the convention center after a few rancid tofurturs (I can't not eat free food) to see if they would take my KISS Army ID, pump my stomach, and sell me some antibiotics. Didn't care if I had to pay rack rate; my guts were four minutes from exploding like a Claymore mine, plus I'd also had an annoying cough for days, couldn't shake it. Epiglottitis. Inflammation of the upper trachea. Horror. Sickness. Death. I'm a pussy about getting sick, but this upper respiratory stuff gets on top of me too fast, which isn't good. The daily subway ride is basically an hour-long bath in tubes of bacteria and viruses for months of the year, and airplanes are even worse.

The clinic was running a free dental clinic in the parking lot, a dozen interns pulling teeth and fitting dentures on a makeshift assembly line, popping molars and drilling holes like a NASCAR pit crew changing tires. The sergeant in charge yelled at the soldiers in a bullhorn. "BRUSH 'EM IF YOU GOT 'EM! TAKE CARE OF YOUR TEETH IN COMBAT SITUATIONS, TROOPS! WE NEED YOU CHEWING SHIT ON A SHINGLE WITH OPTIMUM EFFICIENCY WHEN WE START ANOTHER WAR NEXT WEEK."

I stood in line behind a patient who looked like a Civil War veteran, bleeding from his gums and complaining about his railroad pension. I asked him if he had any antibiotics to sell on the down-low, so maybe I could save some time and skip the day-long queue. He pulled a grimy bag of gas station CBD gummies from the pocket of his dirty cloak. "These magic beans won't get you high, but they're cheaper'n whisky if you get 'em at the flea market. They cured my dog's gout. Maybe they'll work for you."

A woman in pink scrubs with mermaids on them ran up to me and asked me to urgently donate blood. "I NEED BLOOD! You need to sign a waiver saying Jesus is our Lord and Savior and present your voter registration card. We ran out of gift cards to Church's Chicken, but we still have a few cookies. CHILDREN ARE DYING! CHILDREN ARE DY-ING! WE NEED YOUR GOD DAMNED BLOOD FOR JESUS!"

Didn't want to donate, but thought it would be funny if I sang AC/DC's "If You Want Blood (You Got It)" to her. She probably wouldn't get the reference. Also, I read an article recently — it may have been bullshit; every article is — that most of the blood donated to these clinics gets sold overseas, and a hedge fund manager bro rakes it in on the profits. The most valuable exported fluid, by ounce. It's lit-erally vampirism. I didn't want a hole in my arm in exchange for a stale cookie and a Dixie cup of warm orange juice that would give me uncontrollable diarrhea just so some asshole bro fund manager could buy a second yacht. Wasn't there a horror movie in the Eighties about this?

* * *

Speaking of impromptu dental clinics, the Vallejo white power militia group on Meetup.com did a bootleg Invisalign pop-up in the parking lot of the old Shoney's that burned down during a gang shootout. It wasn't the real brand-name Invisalign tooth straightener, but a knock-off kit from China that smelled like spermicidal lubricant and caused third-degree skin burns in one of four patients. (I don't know if you can get skin grafts on your gums, but I'm sure I'll have nightmares thinking about it for the next week.) Affordable prices, until they got arrested. They didn't get nailed for white power stuff; Align Technology, Incorporated filed a preliminary injunction, something about stolen trade secrets. Do not fuck with the Federal Trade Commission.

I hadn't seen sunlight in about two months. Short days, constant rain, miserable weather... No wonder people move to Arizona, even though you have to deal with people who have moved to Arizona. There was a story that week on the local news about someone who bought a full-spectrum light to cure their sadness, and the DEA thought their house was illegally growing weed, so they launched a drone strike, took out the entire neighborhood with Hellfire missiles. I don't need that kind of aggravation in my life. I'll take Prozac, do some aerobics, whatever the hell to avoid getting my apartment firebombed. (Well, I won't do aerobics. I might buy the video tape, and maybe jerk off to it once or twice, but I don't have the motivation to do anything daily. I'm not sure how I've managed to not starve to death at this point.)

Someone down the hall ground up an antique armoire or dresser or something into a fine powder, to mix into soups and gravies as a thickening agent. It was all the rage — internet memes about how horse-based glues and old wood had no calories or carbs or some damn thing. Not only did I have to listen to this asshole run a grinding wheel 24/7 for a week straight, but the airborne dust made my allergies terminal, like in the ten-Benadryl-an-hour range, constant torment, unable to see, eyes swelled up like Rocky after a fight. I was trying to find info online on if it was safe to vape crumbled-up Allegra, but I didn't want to blow out my liver or make my lungs any worse.

I went to bother the neighbor, maybe get him to shut off the 117-decibel electric motor for a few hours every night, but he somehow boarded his door shut from the outside. Must have paid someone on Postmates to do it for him. I didn't really understand his end game here, but I'm not into the low-carb thing, and I'm also not exactly a fan of soup.

Thought about a trip to the apartment rental office to complain, but they were only open 22 minutes a week, and not like in a row, either.

You Can't Force Your Toyota Celica to Enjoy the Low-Carb Lifestyle

This Atkins diet auto service plan is bullshit. Grass-fed flat iron steaks make a poor substitute for brake pads, he realized, as the Toyota skidded through the mall sideways, all safety equipment replaced by meat products. It doesn't matter if your airbags are replaced with protein and fat: you're going to lose the same amount of weight in any car accident if your skin's on fire and your seat belts are made out of bacon strips.

He flew through the shattered windshield and the Celica hood ornament plunged into his forehead, punching a hole through his skull. The memories of a fourth-grade pissing contest and the smell of tangerine-flavored fluoride gel filled his thoughts, a hazy dream about a gang of mystery writers stealing the toilets from his condominium because he refused to check his luggage on the Eastern Airlines flight to Uganda. A Ben Franklin store's mannequin, posed homoerotically with the latest Easter sodomy jacket, broke his fall.

He would wake from the coma ten weeks later, and attempt to strangle a nurse, while screaming "give me a fucking cigarette!" until a Blue Cross claims adjuster and aspiring amateur wrestler put in him a full nelson and choked him into submission. The insurance adjuster tore off his shirt and played shitty Randy Orton entrance music, a sad ballad of shitty Nu Metal guitars and douchey riffage echoing through the tiny speaker of his prepaid phone. Everyone loved the spectacle of power, and a YouTube clip of it went viral and landed him a three-figure endorsement deal from one of those e-cig companies, the ultimate in D-list celebrity fame.

Gary Jerry and the Crying of the Emus

The day's quest: I needed to do a piss test for a stupid factory job, a minimum-wage gig silver-plating shovels and pickaxes for commemorative or ceremonial uses. No worries about pissing hot; this town was too boring to have any good drugs, and I hadn't seen a bagel in months, let alone ones with poppy seeds. My problem was I had to find the hospital, didn't have a map, and didn't want to stop at a gas station and listen to some idiot who dropped out of the third grade lecture me on how book learnin' was useless. I tried to follow the maze of hospital signs around town, which may have been planted by someone who was drunk, or maybe pointed to a hospital that didn't exist anymore.

I don't know why I couldn't remember where the hospital was in town, but I had a vivid memory of being there in 1974, I think. One of my earliest memories, spending four nights in the ICU because my parents thought I was allergic to water, and I drank four glasses that year. (Turns out, my medical issue was because of my kindergarten class full of unvaccinated kids giving each other rabies. I didn't catch rabies; just PTSD. But I think they still called it "shell shock" back then, so they gave me a picture bible and a stern talking-to, and sent me home.)

Finally found the medical clinic that did urine tests, almost by accident. I didn't realize it was just behind Fretwell Park, the place on the river with a park shelter building you could rent for special occasions. Probably a zoning nightmare of a land parcel they couldn't develop into riverfront apartments, so they threw down a jungle gym and a prefab building made with wood beams and a corrugated metal roof. Even in yahoo country, riverfront property had to be worth something, right? Must have been some insane restrictions on the plot to end up making it a cedar chip playground covered in dog shit.

I remember a few family reunions at this park, maybe a birthday or stay-of-execution celebration of some sort. There was a got-out-of-prison party for one of my third cousins almost every week back then. (This was right after the breathalyzer was invented.) It was always the same celebration: shit-kicker country music pumped through a weak Sears stereo, bad egg salad that got everyone sick and usually killed at least one old person, lukewarm Kroger soda in sticky two-liter bottles you did not want to touch, a swimming pool with too much chlorine and too much piss. I think I had a second cousin six times removed that jumped head-first into the shallow end of that concrete pool and broke his neck. Maybe I just dreamed that, I don't know.

I also remember going to that park one of the last times I saw my buddy Glen. He dragged me out to Fretwell for some stupid party that was supposed to be off the hook, and ended up being a bust. His necrophiliacs anonymous group had an annual dance, and he said it was always crawling with pussy, but when we got there, it was like seventeen guys listening to a Foreigner album. It wasn't even a good Foreigner album. I think it was the one from the late 80s, with only lame ballads on it. And no worse place for a bunch of sad mid-tempo ballads than a sausage fest party full of necrophiliacs.

I knew Glen from grade school. His parents were morticians who got locked up for something nefarious when he was in third grade, maybe organ trafficking, but I could never get a straight story from him, except that they were obviously innocent, and he wasn't allowed to visit them at the state Supermax because in the 60s, his dad wrote a Loompanics book about how to break out of Supermax prisons and the feds were convinced any visitors would smuggle in a hacksaw or some gun pieces. Glen's grandparents raised him, and he was the most Satanic of my various Satanic friends. Always wore all black, and had a record player that only played Judas Priest albums backwards.

"I need to split town," Glen said. We wallflowered in the back corner of the dance, drank warm cans of Big K while I considered the logistics of a good murder/suicide without a gun or knife, maybe something involving my belt and one of my shoes as some kind of flail weapon.

"You thinking of going away to that trade school for grave digging out in Missoula next semester? I thought you had to finish your GED first."

"No, I mean right after we're done here. Like, tonight. I need to leave the state immediately, if you can give me a lift to the Amtrak station. I've got a zoning problem. I want to build a house on the lake, but they're giving me shit about the easement. Said they want to expand the highway to four lanes, and I'd have to get new septic put in or something. I didn't even mention the fallout shelter I started to build underground in the backyard. I'm sure they'll give me unending shit about that, too."

This whole fucking city is a zoning problem, I thought. Last year, the zoning commission tried to pass a law saying every new house built needed the Ten Commandments somewhere on the property, and it barely got shut down by the ACLU. "I didn't know you owned land." I also didn't know how he'd ever afford to build a house, but I didn't want to ask too many questions.

"Yeah, I've got this acre and a half up near the marina next to six-span bridge. It was my great-uncle's. He died in 1961 in a tornado, and his vacant house got arsoned ten years later. Someone was reading about Ed Gein, thought Uncle Charlie may have had some dead bodies up there, so they torched the place. He totally didn't, although he did have a basement full of mannequins, mostly stolen from Ben Franklin stores. A few Sears ones, but nothing racy. These ones didn't even have heads or arms on them. They're so realistic now, they're practically like Real Dolls. I saw a mannequin at Victoria's Secret the other day and I swear the goddamn thing had labia. Anyway, I inherited the place, been trying to do something with the land, and it's been nothing but legal bullshit. Endless paperwork, they say I need a permit and then they don't issue it, all that garbage. So I'm selling the land and moving to Las Vegas."

"Aren't you on probation? I didn't think you could leave the state." Glen had a shoplifting problem, and got nicked shoving Testors model paints in his jeans at the Hobby Lobby out next to the dildo factory south of town. He doesn't build model airplanes, and you can barely get high off that stuff anymore, since they changed the formulation. I don't even think he realized he did it. Six months of paperwork and piss tests, though — total hassle.

"More legal bullshit. I'm sure they won't miss me, but try to keep this to yourself. I'll get in touch when I get out there. Hey, do you think before we go to the train station, we can hit the Perkins? All of the food here looks like it would give the living dead a case of diarrhea, and I'm planning on spending the next three or four days on a train with minimal bathroom facilities, if you know what I mean."

"Yeah, let's hit the fuckin' road," I said, quoting *Blue Velvet*, not that you could even rent a David Lynch movie in this town. We stole a family-sized box of store-brand Chex mix, loaded into my piece of shit car, and quickly exited the party. No nitrous tank in the car, unfortunately, so we couldn't go Frank Booth-style. Maybe we'd find some Pabst Blue Ribbon later on.

* * *

Glen didn't drive. Didn't believe in it. He wasn't Amish or anything, he just didn't think he ever needed to learn about it. His grandfather was a pipeline supervisor who commuted to Oklahoma and back every month. It turned out that he had three different families in various cities along the I-44 corridor between Wichita Falls, Texas and St. Louis, Missouri. I think this fucked with Glen's head somewhat, along with his dad being locked up. It's also probably why his grandpa never had money, and Glen had to fend for himself by shoplifting and robbing graves.

We listened to *...And Justice for All* on the drive to Perkins. I was stuck on old Metallica that week, some stupid nostalgia thing. Or maybe I had nothing better in the car; there were several rust holes in the floorboards, and I lost a lot of cassettes over the years. "Didn't these assholes cut their hair and start collecting Picasso paintings and thousand-dollar wine?" he said.

"Picasso wouldn't surprise me. They made so goddamn much money off that *Smell the Glove* album, they can probably afford to hunt humans from helicopters."

"Sure, but that doesn't mean I want to listen to their music." He ejected the cassette from the deck and threw it out the window, hanging onto a piece of the tape so it completely unspooled into a giant 421.875-foot long streamer behind the car. "You got any Sabbath in this piece of shit?"

* * *

I've probably covered enough "eating at Denny's" stories in all of my other books that I could phone in the part of the story where we go to a diner to eat and waste three hours of time in the middle of the night. Key highlights: the town was too shitty to have a Denny's, so we got a Perkins instead, which is like a restaurant not being able to afford Coke or Pepsi, so they only serve RC Cola. Glen ordered too much food, then stiffed me with the check, but that's fine; I had a job, he didn't. He also spent most of the meal trying to smoke at the table, but we were in the no-smoking section. This was at the point in history when they would make half of the restaurant no-smoking, because obviously having an invisible line through the middle of the dining area would make one half completely impenetrable from any airborne contaminants, right? And since everyone in town smoked, they always ran out of room in the smoking section and put smokers in non-smoking booths, where they would light up anyway.

"What happened to that job you had?" I picked at my sampler platter, wondering how many years it was going to take off my life. "I thought you were making like twenty-five bucks an hour for pressing a button all day. Was it some kind of RV assembly gig?"

"No, it was a torture device factory." Glen tore apart an empty pack of Camels to find all the secret Freemason messages ("LaRouche Says Masonry Funds Terrorism!"). "They made torture devices: waterboarding tables, ball-crushers, and limb-spreaders for enhanced interrogation black sites, mostly. Law enforcement officials only, but they did a mix of federal and local contracts. Business really picked up in the Reagan years. The actual work was drill press, punch press, stamping edges on steel pieces, the usual light machinery shit. It sucked, but work is work, so it's going to suck. Anyone who gives you that 'find a job you love' bullshit is fucking delusional and probably has a hidden brain tumor. And you didn't press a button — it had two buttons — it's a safety interlock system, so you can't put your hand in a 200-ton press when you're drunk. It must be some OSHA requirement, because I'm sure it costs at least twelve dollars to add that second switch, and this place couldn't even afford toilet paper in their shitter."

"Man, they could have made millions selling that stuff to S&M perverts. Once a weirdo starts building a dungeon in your basement and locks in with the project, they're constantly dumping your life's savings into new over-engineered restraints and chains and whatnot."

"Maybe that shit's popular out in big cities on the coasts, but freaks here are probably still in the closet, trading polaroids over snail mail and putting coded ads in the back of the penny saver. That one porno store in town can't legally sell sex toys — it's in the state constitution. You either have to drive sixty miles to jerk off, or improvise, build it out of food from Kroger's and home-improvement supplies from the True Value."

"You want to avoid going to Ace Hardware or you'll get that song stuck in your head. And good luck fucking out your neighbor with a piece of PVC pipe wrapped in liver. Great way to get salmonella of the b-hole, or some kind of plastic-induced colon cancer."

"No shit. Anyway, I worked with this guy named Gary Jerry, this bowl cut motherfucker who was way too into NASCAR and rustic furniture. He lost all his money on an emu scam. Some Mennonites went door-to-door all over town, getting people to put money down on these things."

"Emo scam? Like those mopey assholes listening to The Smiths and Depeche Mode?"

"No, *emu*, with a U. It's a weird bird with long legs, like an ostrich. They farm emus, like for meat. They sell a starter kit with a bitch or two and a bull, maybe some special food pellets or whatever, everything to get 'em fucking and shitting out babies you can butcher. Gary Jerry went on and on about how they had more vitamin C in the meat per pound than a bag of oranges, you could raise a hundred of them on an acre of land, no cholesterol, all that shit. Something about Ford making a car out of emu flesh back during the war, the government shutting it down and putting it in a secret warehouse with the Ark of the Covenant. You could print books and newspapers on emu paper, and they'd last a thousand years. Emu oil cured cancer, stopped epilepsy, was more healthy than fuckin' grapefruits and jogging. Whatever. He must have heard all of this on an episode of the Joe Rogan podcast. So Gary Jerry cashes out his pension, buys a gaggle or pack or herd of these fuckin' birds— what the fuck is a bunch of emus?"

"Mob. A group of emus is called a mob." I don't know how I knew this. I must have paid attention to fifteen minutes of biology class in my freshman year.

"That's so fuckin' metal," he said. "OK, so he buys a *mob* of emus and fences in his trailer park lot so he can fatten them up for the slaughter. Won't shut up about it, brings in polaroids every day of how big they're getting, talks like he's hit the lottery and he's going to sell this meat for beaucoup bucks. He comes in a month or two later, covered in sores, like he got attacked by a weed-eater in hand to hand combat. Says he lost all the emus. The city was going to fine him $500 a day per emu, for not having a food permit. Fucking zoning laws."

"So what, did he have to murder them all?"

"Well, he wanted to. But his nephew who also lived in his trailer was a big acid head, used to work out at the Maxi Mart on county road 18, and got fired for huffing gas fumes on the clock. Anyway, he'd been feeding these fucking things codeine cough syrup, because he saw some Greenpeace thing about the plight of aviary sanctuaries or some shit, wanted to cheer up the birds. So when Gary Jerry went out there with a gas-powered hedge trimmer to chop their heads off, but they all went nuts, started having hallucinations, tripping balls on codeine, and went fucking berserker on him. He's in this wire mesh cage, close-combat swinging that Toro trimmer, these birds throwing talons into him, feathers everywhere. Almost all of the birds got away, but he was totally decimated from their berserker mode pecking attack."

"If you listen to fools, the mob rules. Fuckin' Dio, man."

"No shit. And Gary Jerry had like two or three birds that survived, but he couldn't sell the meat. So he brings in like a hundred pounds of emu steaks, and he's trying to sell them at lunch on the down-low. I tried some — I mean, what the hell, he was giving away emu nuggers, might as well. But they were all full of pieces of barbed wire and dog shit, and the flesh is nasty as it is. It's like eating a catcher's mitt that's been left in your back yard all winter."

"Did he make any of the emu oil? Can you score us any?" I had high cholesterol, and maybe it would cure gout or something. I didn't know what the stuff tasted like, or if you were supposed to cook french fries with it or what, but I figured it wouldn't hurt to have a jar around the house, just in case.

"Hell no. He's way out of business, like Toys R Us out of business. Gary Jerry lost everything he owned. His wife maxed out his credit cards, hocked all his tools and appliances, and took off with his car and dog. He couldn't afford his trailer anymore, had to move in with his brother. Then his brother's trailer burned down — arson, or maybe he fell asleep smoking — so he's living in a ditch at the edge of town, walking everywhere and showering once a week at the YMCA. He tried punching a hole in his hand for workman's comp, but like I said, safety interlock. Tried to work one of the switches with his dick while his hand was in the press, but he was too short to get it to work, and when he got caught, they fired him. Every semi-skilled machine job in the city that wasn't union all hired from the same labor staffing place, which blacklisted him, and he was too ugly to work in fast food. He was going to get a job with the census, but he couldn't find his birth certificate or something. I don't know what happened to him. Moral of the story: you get what you pay for, or something."

We sat at the Perkins for a few more hours, until it was time for him to catch the first train out of town. I didn't know if I would ever see Glen again, but he was too weird to vanish forever. I knew at some point a month or a year from now, I'd probably get a random phone call from him telling me he needed me to drive to Chicago and bail him out of jail, or describing his philosophy on the designated-hitter rule and ass-eating. There was a slight fear he would end up dead in the desert, suckered into a shotgun wedding, or locked in federal pound-you-in-the-ass prison for crimes he definitely did commit. But I hoped he would be back someday.

* * *

Anyway — that hospital — I went in to take the piss test. I knew it was going to go south because instead of being owned by Kaiser or Beacon or some university, this place was operated by KFC. Awesome hospital food — you could get a bucket of chicken in your bed after major cardiac surgery, and they would even do a feeding tube of gravy. But for actual medical care, I had my doubts.

They didn't have the setup where you took a leak and put the plastic jar in a little glory hole specimen tray thing built into the wall. A nurse had to actually watch you take a piss. And it wasn't that the nurse had to be like in the same room as the bathroom; they actually had to have two eyes on your dick as you completed the deposit, start to finish.

It would have been bad enough if it was just some dumb obese murse with a neck-beard who wanted to talk about Notre Dame football while I tried to eke out a pee. It turned out the only nurse on duty was an ex-girlfriend from high school, who I hadn't seen in like a decade. Seeing her was like revisiting the scene where I almost got killed in a car wreck, except for the part where I had my cock out in front of a urinal, holding a little plastic cup.

This was a woman who I thought for some stupid reason I would spend my life with, and in the few months I dated her, she managed to fuck all twenty-eight past, present, and future members of the band Warrant. Everyone in the universe except me knew this. She was even such a completist that she fucked Chris Vincent, who played bass for only like the first two months of the band's history, and Scott Warren, who I think was in the band for less than a year and only played harmonica. I think she actually fucked Vincent and Warren at the same time.

While I stood with dick in hand, she told me all about how she studied nursing at some religious school in Iowa or Idaho or something, because you didn't have to take any science classes there. I kept thinking about the improbability of having a nurse staring at my cock and it was one she was already familiar with, albeit she was also familiar with the members of every member of Warrant.

She started showing me school pictures of her grandkids and as I did the math about how she could already have grandkids in grade school, my entire urinary tract was as dry as an abandoned well in the deserts of the wild west. I gave up, zipped up, left, and found another job selling kitchen knives door to door.

Easy Money

...The thick smell of gasoline vapor from the chopped and dropped truck in front of me at the intersection, a too-rich tri-carb setup dumping raw fuel in the air at an alarming rate. They had the foot-wide slicks on the back, the shaved trim, the chromed naked-lady tail light covers, everything but a fresh coat of paint on the rust-and-bondo body. The kids call it "patina" now, charge an extra five grand and use a special acid mix to eat rust into the metal, make it look like your car's been sitting in a field for twenty years. I know, old man yells at sky, what's the deal with pre-ripped jeans that cost a hundred bucks. I guess there's a reason I'm not rich, right?

It took another fifty minutes and nine seconds, the exact length of the Van Hagar tape in the player, to circle the lake. Winding roads, twisting trees, the roots undercutting the concrete, adding a ripple effect like natural speed bumps in the asphalt. I got to the cottage just in time to see the garage sale end. The last of the good stuff gone, the old man dragged his remaining items from the driveway to his garage: broken jelly jars, collectible plastic cutlery, and plastic trays stolen from various fast food restaurants. If it still snowed in this part of the country (global warming) they might be useful as sleds, but I could always steal one myself. And I had no real need for a fair-condition Burger Chef tray, although this is the part of the country where people collect things like manhole covers, telephone poles, and cinder blocks from department stores, so who knows, maybe I did.

"When I worked at the old RCA factory, my only job for fifty-five years was dumping harmful chemicals down a storm drain. Told us it wouldn't hurt anything, but they also said smoking ten packs a day made you grow big and strong, too." He showed me the artificial spleen strapped to his belt, an ancient Delco model from the 60s, a bakelite case and transistor amps. "I think they worked on time travel there, Nazi scientists from the war, some kind of fourth-dimensional low-frequency beam. You think those Terminator movies could be true?"

"That bit with the Atari pocket computer breaking into ATMs was obvious bullshit," I said. "And every time they had someone new play the kid, they'd end up going insane. But maybe that was from the time travel, who knows."

"I love money laundering. I don't love laundry, and I don't even really love money, after a lifetime of having to make and save and spend it. But give me a strap of fake twenties, and I'll go to a hundred corner stores buying packs of gum and candy bars so I can get back $19.43 in change. God damn, it's better than getting your rocks off with a girl..."

A Lamborghini zipped past at high speed, nearly clipping my car. "What the fuck was wrong with that dude's engine? That car sounded like a lawn mower."

"That's a Fiero with a bunch of shit glued to the side. Kit car. Ol' Dale Stevens, he lives off Conklin Road, in that house that looks like a god damn shoebox with windows. He's a doctor in Chicago, made all his money writing fake scripts for pain pills to gang bangers. Says he's a surgeon, but the only thing he's operated on is my patience. Driving that god damned imposter go-kart. It doesn't even have the right emblems on it. The bull is backwards. Real ones are illegal, I guess. Can't even find them on the dark web…"

I drove back to town and had to look up the tape — did you know that first Van Hagar album was a bigger pull on the Billboard charts than the last real Van Halen album with Diamond Dave? Every Van Hagar album topped out at #1 on the charts, and none of the Diamond Dave albums did. That's some bullshit. Yet another perfect example of why I need to hack into the NORAD computers and launch a 10,000-warhead nuclear attack on our own country. Maybe I can do it with an Atari Portfolio handheld computer like John Connor. Time to hit eBay, look for a working specimen.

I Like My Coffee Like I Like my Men

Vice President Jeffrey L. Dahmer gave a two-hour press conference on the latest financial meltdown, although he answered no questions and gave no details on anything about the economy. Instead, he spent the first hour talking about how to fuck the stab wounds in a corpse, and the best way to cook a severed head with only a low-watt rental apartment microwave. Most of the second hour was him riffing about the new *Star Wars* movie, and all of the reporters left during that, because the last time a journalist accidentally posted a spoiler to one of those J.J. Abrams-directed shit-fests, a group of beardo George Lucas apologists firebombed the Washington Post headquarters and burned the building to the ground. At the end of the press conference he told everyone to buy savings bonds and always use Ozium air sanitizer spray to cover up the stench of corpses rotting in your apartment.

ONE, TWO, THREE, FLOOR

Mountain Dew Meal Replacement Drink offered a thousand dollars to anyone who would get killed lying down on the pavement in the high-speed motorcycle lane of the I-5 corridor. Send a selfie of your corpse in the road, and they'd Venmo a grand to your phone. Seventeen deaths in the first week, and they didn't have to pay out a single victim, because nobody read the fine print in the contest rules. (Item #768 in the contest rules and regulations said all photos had to conform to the CIE 1931 color space, and I don't think there are any cell phones that shoot in anything but sRGB.) But mission accomplished: everyone in the country knew about the new drink, and it was cheaper than a single ad buy at three in the morning on a local UHF station.

* * *

The XFL announced yet another reboot. This time, every player would be left-handed, a rarity in football. Vince McMahon said it was in tribute to Owen Hart, but it probably had to do with under-paying players that couldn't get drafted in the NFL. Right-wing idiots immediately assumed it was a political thing and promised boycotts and violence.

Vegas gave the over/under at two games played, maybe three if they got a cable deal and the cheerleaders were topless.

* * *

Day 266 of the Gene Simmons assassination crisis stretched on, inexplicably covered 24/7 on the country news channel because of a Viacom license dispute over the rights for KISS music. The accused, with the obligatory triple-barreled name Kenneth Wayne Cook, allegedly brought a sniper rifle to the band's 17th reunion show in some random outdoor arena in Tennessee or Arkansas or something, set up in a eight hundred-dollar seat (all he could afford) which was actually in the parking lot across the street, and took out the long-tongued musician at a range of about two thousand meters.

This week's news coverage was a long argument about the Canadian Army McMillan TAC-50 .50-caliber sniper rifle he used. The prosecutor mistakenly called it an anti-personnel rifle, and Cook's defense team argued it was an anti-materiel and anti-personnel rifle, and the entire case should be thrown out. The KISS merchandise licensing team was busy trying to find a way to legally sell commemorative KISS sniper rifles at a 400% markup. Maybe they could re-move the firing pin or weld a chunk of metal in the barrel, and put a picture of Gene on the lower receiver. (Just a sticker; it would cut into the profit margin too much if it was engraved.)

"We don't want to promote the assassination of band members of seventies arena rock bands who try to make a comeback, but the stock market is up by seven percent this week." The president, actually a hologram of Sonny Bono transmitted onto a donor body pulled from a medical lab, didn't tell people to go shoot members of The Eagles or Steely Dan, but he didn't exactly tell them not to, either. It was all business. It's why they banned falafel, made the hot dog the national sandwich.

* * *

A representative from Douglas Aircraft time-traveled from 1954 to tell the aeronautical community that the Nintendo Switch was bullshit. "I've got slide-rule calculations. I helped build a never-launched military space station. We should be starting another war in Vietnam. Maybe design our own supersonic airliner." Someone from the press corps interrupted him, and explained how his company merged with McDonnell aircraft, then merged with Boeing, and later was bought by Nintendo for R&D purposes (although this was probably a money-laundering scheme). He apologized, then went to a men's room and drank a gallon of shoe polish he stole from an airport shoeshine stand, before jumping in front of a moving train.

The Sixty-First Parallel Wormhole Debacle

Lars wrote me an email about how he invented the Vodka-Mucil and drank five every day now. He would mix together two heaping tablespoons of fiber powder, eight ounces of cheap vodka that's sold in a plastic jug, and a twist of lime. Shaken, not stirred. He was trying to trademark the name, but ran into some obscure loophole-slash-problem, like he had to fly to Italy to print one copy of a fake package and drink it in a public place, something about them not observing a pre-WW2 international copyright treaty, and that's why Chef Boyardee canned ravioli can allegedly contain up to 47% rat poisoning. I'm sure Procter and Gamble has good lawyers, so I didn't argue this in my reply back to him.

I reported on today's office drama: Sandwich Bob got arrested for counterfeiting. Sandwich Bob sold sandwiches in my building (not by the seashore), pushing a little cart in a lap around each floor every day. His inventory usually included plastic-wrapped roach coach food, Wise potato chips and every once in a while, some expired Little Debbie snack cakes. He occasionally had some good stuff, not just lunch meat and tuna salad on white bread. I think the first time I ever had avocado or pesto was from Sandwich Bob's cart. (We didn't have vegetables back in Indiana when I grew up.

I think guacamole is still a class B misdemeanor in some counties.)

The thought of Bob selling bootleg lottery tickets on the side made no sense. Honestly, I didn't think he was smart enough to know how to print fake lottery tickets, like with the scratch-off silver stuff. Maybe he bought them from a customer or a brother-in-law with a printing press. He never tried to sell me one, but people always think I'm a cop, even though I look nothing like a cop. The whole thing smelled like a set-up. Maybe the office management company hated him, or they wanted a cut of the sandwich money. Or it could have been some bigger thing, like Sandwich Bob owed the mafia. Who knows.

Anyway, I would miss his London broil roast beef sandwiches with Colby cheese and horseradish sauce. They replaced him with some food truck foodie asshole who only sold Rocky Mountain oyster tacos with kimchi, and I'm definitely not eating that with a single toilet per floor in the office. I'm not industrious enough to pack my lunch, so I'd need to leave the office every day to grab something to eat.

The Billy Sill Sound of Jersey played in the background, while I drove through residential streets — speed bump city — avoiding the parking lot of I-5. I lived on sweet and sour chicken back then, bought a gallon at a time from the crap takeout spot next to the Leather Daddy Safeway. I forget why we called it the Leather Daddy Safeway — I think there was a cashier who always wore assless chaps and had his significant other on a leash as he rang up groceries. I do miss those days. You won't get that kind of service with a self-checkout line.

If my car had enough juice from the dashboard wiring, I'd mount a travel microwave under the glove box, heat up a pint of the radioactive orange sauce and chunks, suck down a thousand calories on the hour-long, two-mile drive home every day. But West German ingenuity from the seventies was in full effect here, the whole car accessory system running on a measly amp of current in the thin wire coming through the firewall. The little Alpine amp I had hidden under the dash would make the headlights dim every time I turned up the Motörhead past three on the dial.

I cut through someone's muddy backyard, popped out in a small suburb an hour north of town, a place with a park-and-ride for the commuter busses, a bunch of strip malls, and lots of identical apartment buildings. I struggled against the surface road traffic until I found the last remaining Kenny Rogers Roasters chicken location in the US. It was kept running because of some lawsuit, although they sold very little chicken, and a Vietnamese family ran a Cambodian buffet in the dining room. Odd choice, given the history between those two countries, but maybe Cambodian food is cheaper.

(Oh, also, Kenny Rogers Roasters is still thriving in Malaysia and the Philippines. I also stumbled across a location when I was at the Sahara Center Mall in Dubai. It's worth it if you happen to be in the United Arab Emirates for another reason, but I wouldn't fly twelve hours just to eat there. That Taco Bell day spa trip damn near killed me. I think I still have a lump or a calcium deposit on one of my vertebrae from those "economy select" seats. No amount of cheap massage is going to work that one loose.)

In the parking lot, I was accosted by a guy who looked like Carlos Castillo Armas, the Guatemalan dictator installed by a CIA coup in the fifties. One of my favorite toys as a kid was this "CIA's Greatest Hits" playing cards, and I guess I accidentally memorized the identities of 52 CIA strongmen and double-agents before I started Kindergarten. I was pretty sure he got shot in the head by a leftist sympathizer in like '57, but here he was, trying to sell five-dollar candy bars for a grade school DARE anti-drug program. Didn't look a day over 40, and he was still rocking the Hitler mustache he had back in the fifties. I told him I did not want any candy bars five times, then finally told him I was off sugar and he backed off. It's a felony to argue with someone over their dietary restrictions in this town.

A bathroom visit was a point of urgency for me, but they didn't have one, just a urinal which was next to a deep fat fryer on the back line, and I imagined if I whipped it out, I'd probably get hit by spatter from a batch of french fries or whatever they called their chicken nuggets there. (Kenny nuggets, I don't know.) The assistant manager told me there was an experimental portal next to the grease dumpster out back connected to a set of underground tunnels leading to a mall about a quarter-mile across the highway. I didn't know what he meant by "experimental," but I bought a five-pound bucket of the nuggets (no sweet-and-sour chicken, unfortunately) and went to find the restroom.

I popped the hatch, and carefully traversed a greasy metal ladder into a massive underground complex probably built during the Sixties by Boeing or Teledyne to keep a mall running as a contingency after a nuclear war. (Climbing down a grease-encrusted set of rungs while holding five pounds of chicken in one hand is a lot harder than it sounds.) The tunnel complex reminded me of the movie *THX-1138* except there was nobody there, and I didn't have a bald haircut. After about ten minutes of walking in the concrete labyrinth, eating nuggets and daydreaming about recording an ambient album in the massive echo chamber, I realized I was completely lost. There were cryptic numbers spray-painted with stencils on the concrete near each ladder or hatch, but the numbering system made no sense, and looked like random UPC codes to grocery products or ZIP+4 codes. They weren't even in order. I'd never make it back from lunch on time, not that I ever gave a fuck about that.

Something resembling an exit appeared on one of the walls, or at least I hoped it was an exit and not a passage leading straight into a giant chipper/shredder tube. I climbed the ladder for about ten minutes straight (a bit easier now that the chicken was gone), opened a hatch, and emerged back to the surface. It was dusk outside, and I was in the parking lot of a Fred Meyer, no idea where, except it was amazingly cold outside, all of a sudden. I went to the doors of the hypermart, and saw I was in Anchorage, Alaska. Across the street was the Sears Mall, which no longer had a Sears, and didn't have much of a mall in the first place, either. I had no idea what prestidigitation or supernatural force caused me to teleport 2,260 miles in what I thought was twenty or so minutes. Maybe I walked that far while I was eating the nuggets and lost track of time, I don't know. I tend to black out after eating like 133.3333 chicken nuggets. (That's only an estimate. I'm sure they short-changed me at least a dozen nuggets. And they only gave me two sauce packets.)

* * *

Trading long emails daily at an office job probably dates me a bit. This was a habit I developed before social media beat the attention span out of all of us, at a time where you either sent long thousand-word dispatches in a copy of Eudora, played FreeCell, or actually did your job. (And they locked all of us out of FreeCell after the IT department got metrics on how basically 37% of the entire company's time was spent flipping 16-bit digital cards onto different stacks.) But my group of friends must have written *War and Peace* ten times over on a monthly basis with long diatribes about absolutely nothing via the email tubes.

Like I remember at some point, Lars became obsessed with AstroTurf. I don't remember why he had an unnatural affinity with the AstroDome, maybe something about his time living in Houston as a male exotic dancer. But one week, he pulled up patents on the original Monsanto product called Chemgrass. Then he fell down this k-hole about the first outdoor use of AstroTurf, a year after the Astro-Dome, was the Indiana State University stadium in Terre Haute, Indiana, where thirty-some years later, Timothy McVeigh would be executed. Then the floodgates opened: studies on knee injuries from artificial playing surfaces; an attempt at correlating Unabomber targets with universities that used artificial turf; a cut subplot from the *Brady Bunch* about how their back yard was fake grass because Mike Brady had a college roommate who came back from the war in Vietnam addled with PTSD and started a landscaping company, and Brady hired him to install the artificial lawn.

What eventually got him off the AstroTurf kick was that the McRib came back, and he was insistent on seeing if he could eat the boneless pork sandwich in as few bites as possible. He wanted to see if it was possible to get the entire sandwich through his digestive system in one piece. I don't remember the exact number, but it seems like he got it down to less than a dozen bites, maybe like seven or eight. This included the bun, but he did take the pickles off, because that would be just plain disgusting.

* * *

At least Fred Meyer had a decent bathroom and sold coats. There wasn't much in variety coat-wise, mostly stuff like Coleman hunting jackets, in the kind of camo pattern that said "I have six homeschooled kids and a crippling addiction to chewing tobacco." I found a solid red jacket, and also bought two pounds of fun-sized Snickers and a cold 128-ounce bottle of Coke. The nuggets must have had about a pound of sodium in them, and I knew I'd need some hydration and sugar reinforcement for the impending crash. I also got a bottle of store-brand Tylenol, which was Kroger brand, and I totally forgot that Kroger owned Fred Meyer and thought I'd fallen down a second wormhole. The cashier had a pair of samurai swords strapped to his back, and largely ignored me as he rang me up. I wanted to ask him to cut the tags off my jacket, but didn't want to start an incident.

By the time I got back outside, the portal, my only connection back to Seattle, was gone, missing, vanished. Maybe it was lost, paved over — I don't know. I couldn't find it in the darkness of early night, and it looked like I would have to pay for my own way home. It had been over a decade since I was in Anchorage, so I had no idea how I'd get to the airport and book a one-way flight home. I vaguely knew the airport was west, but that's about it. It was probably too late to catch a flight back to the mainland anyway, so I gave up and walked to the nearest hotel. It was full of work trucks, giant Ford 4x4's with extended cabs, extended beds, extended wheels, extended suspensions, and they took up sixteen parking spaces each. I figured a place full of contractors like that would have cheap rates, since those guys probably couldn't afford an expensive room after filling up their 200-gallon gas tanks every hour.

The place was tragically empty, like the hotel in *The Shining* empty. Nobody's in Alaska before Memorial Day, and judging by the skies and the temperature, it was way before that. Got a room with no problem, no deposit, no credit card hold. The clerk, a sleepy-looking college kid with thick glasses, gave me a cleaning staff skeleton key and told me to pick any room I wanted, because the whole damn place was empty, and the trucks outside belonged to guys who froze to death working on the pipeline, and their corpses wouldn't be removable from the frozen tundra until July. He gave me a whole week for the same price as a single night at rack rate, so fuck it — I decided to make a vacation of the thing. I already bought the jacket, might as well get some use out of it.

The inside of the hotel didn't have a restaurant or a cafe, just a booth next to the front desk selling granola bars that had solidified into bricks, and the booth was closed. The lobby looked like the set of a 1970s science fiction movie, a space hotel covered in groovy wood trim with orange carpet on the walls. I went outside, braved the cold, wandered the "downtown" area, every zipper on my new coat fastened as much as possible to prevent hypothermia.

First impression was that Anchorage was really bizarre. Post-apocalyptic. It was absolutely empty, and a strange orange-gold color filtered through the sky, like a forest fire was happening in the distance. This was a town of 300,000 and it felt like maybe 10,000 were actually around. The hotel was in "downtown" but there was nothing around it, just empty storefronts and abandoned tourist traps boarded up for the winter. I went into food-hunting mode, and absolutely nothing registered on my radar, like a neutron bomb had been detonated overhead. Yelp showed zero places to eat from horizon to horizon, except for a gas station 48 miles away that served hot dogs, and it was closed. There were a few homeless wandering around, but it was totally Omega Man otherwise. And there was the strangest juxtaposition of a fifteen-story hotel, then nothing but empty one-story storefronts for six blocks, then another vacant hotel, the lights on and the heat running so the pipes wouldn't explode. This was all framed by snow-capped mountains in the far distance, which were a strange silver-gray in the night.

I eventually found dinner at a Chinese restaurant, probably the only one in the entire state. It looked like it was perpetually trapped in 1974, with chop suey and horribly racist caricatures on the menu. They did have my beloved sweet and sour chicken, so I got a gallon of that, and endured the weak tea and tasteless entrees, like the rubber wonton soup and egg rolls that were obviously La Choy stuff bought in bulk at Sam's Club. An entire family-sized sharing meal plus a Coke was only $7 with tax. I had them box up the leftovers, even though my room didn't have a microwave and leftovers are generally bullshit. You never know when it's going to snow ten feet overnight and the whole thing goes Uruguayan Rugby team and you have to start eating dead people. The orange sauce would come in handy for that.

* * *

What do you do in Alaska when it isn't the tourist season and you don't enjoy crippling cold, drinking alone, or smoking weed? I had no idea. (I also didn't see a lot of places selling weed. I thought it would be like Denver, where 74% of all businesses are now dispensaries. I think I saw one weed store in Anchorage, but it may have just been a weird t-shirt store, and it was closed.) I wandered the desolate town as much as I could, but after you see the state's only escalator and the place that sells reindeer hot dogs with cream cheese applied with a caulking gun, there's not a lot else to do.

I thought about writing, but I always think about writing and I don't do anything about it. My excuse this time was that I didn't have a computer with me, and the hotel didn't put stationery in the rooms. (The clerk said the owners didn't believe in writing or something.) Typing a book on my phone wasn't going to cut it. During one of my five-mile hikes to the local Target (the only thing open, really) I bought a $99 laptop, but it ran Red Star OS, the operating system used by the North Korean government, and the keyboard was like 92% full-sized, which meant I missed 92% of the keystrokes I tried to make. The plastic laptop lasted for about a thousand words into a book I was trying to start, which was probably a good thing, because take a look at any of the books I've written. It fortunately broke into pieces and I threw it in the garbage.

Bottom line: don't vacation in Alaska out-of-season. Even if you are there right before the season starts and the 18-hour nights don't make you hang yourself, you have to deal with the insufferable bone-crushing cold, and absolutely nothing being open. I wasted an entire day walking five miles to go to a 7-Eleven that was only open from noon to three, for fuck's sake. Plus the cable at the hotel was out — their satellite dish had blown away in a storm — so I couldn't do the usual of watching the same Meg Ryan movie with 20 minutes of commercials per five minutes of content, like I always do when I'm stuck in a hotel. I spent all week in bed, with every blanket in the hotel on top of me, praying for death. I ate at the Chinese place every day, until they banned me for unknown reasons, forcing me to brave the cold and hike back to the Fred Meyer for my own frozen food, which I cooked on top of the room's ancient tube TV, by blocking every vent with blankets and dirty socks until it overheated.

* * *

I spent the last forty-eight hours of my trip packing up, getting ready to leave. It was amazing that I brought exactly zero with me, just the clothes on my back, and a week later, I didn't know how I would jettison enough stuff to get down to two fifty-pound bags plus a carry-on. I made so many trips to Target and CVS, I bought enough garbage to survive three pandemics and a zombie apocalypse. I had endless dumb Alaska t-shirts with epic airbrushed pictures of wolves and bears and eagles and wolves fighting bears and eagles attacking wolves and all of them eating fish the size of Jaws. The shirts were nine for twenty dollars at the only gift shop in town still open, and would last for exactly one wash. I also had almost an entire drug store of pain relievers, sleep medications, medical instruments, wound care products, and even one of those heart defibrillation machines, which I don't even remember buying. I'd probably throw out half of the shirts and maybe the snake bite kit and machete. And maybe half of the sixteen tactical flashlights I bought would end up being a gift to the cleaning staff.

Of course, after two days of packing and almost no sleep the night before, it took an hour and a half for an Uber to show up. I still got to the airport two hours before check-in, but luckily there's a Wendy's in Terminal A. Maybe not luckily — eating three Baconator sandwiches right before a long flight isn't exactly advisable. But it would keep me warm for the entire trip, I guess.

While I wandered the concourses, Lars sent me 167 emails about a job opportunity he found in Antarctica, which sounded like a multi-level marketing scam, but I didn't want to burst his bubble. He planned out how he was going to give away everything he owned, move down there with only a small bag of clothes and some beef jerky, and write a series of get-rich-quick books targeting old people. His theory is he'd sell more copies if they were in large print like those *Reader's Digest* special issues you find at the optometrist, and it would involve less writing. It wasn't a bad plan, but I would have at least brought a CD player and the first six Black Sabbath albums.

I replied back, told him I accidentally did the identical thing and was freezing to death in a climate that was absolutely unbearable, but probably a hundred degrees warmer than it was at McMurdo Station. I didn't tell him that I bought $1600 of garbage at gift shops and gadget stores. If he wanted to do this stupid plan, he needed to find out if they shipped a fixed amount of cargo down to the South Pole as part of the job contract, and then fill that allowance with barter-worthy items up to the very last ounce. "I'm sure if you cornered the market for cigs or pornography down there, you'd make far more money than you would on your salary," I said.

* * *

A long time ago I was playing some game on the PlayStation 2 — it was *Medal of Honor* or *Soldier of Fortune* or *Call of Duty* or *Fucker of Guns* or something where you had to shoot a bunch of Nazis who yelled the same six German words at you. (This was back when killing Nazis was universally acceptable, which dates me somewhat.) Anyway, I was standing in exactly the wrong place at the wrong time when a grenade was thrown or something exploded near me, and I ended up *outside* the video game. The game was designed so that every level you had to complete was a maze of sorts, and all of the "walls" in the maze were detailed on the inside to look like buildings in Germany with bullet holes and Nazi flags and so forth. When I was thrown by that exploding grenade, my character was on the *other* side of the walls. I could see the back sides of these pieces of scenery, and I was running around this completely white null-land that looked like the inside of The Matrix. Off in the distance, there were these pillars of smoke coming out of nowhere, there to contribute to the background when inside the game. I ran around for an hour, looking at the inside-out scenery and wondering if there was anything else cool I could do. I eventually couldn't figure out how to continue, so I had to restart the PlayStation and probably go back to running over prostitutes in *Grand Theft Auto*.

This strange alternate reality was a metaphor for something both me and Lars were always trying to chase, although I don't entirely know what the metaphor is, or how we'd accomplish it. The difference between me and Lars though was that we were trying to break into this *Twilight Zone* dimension in different ways. He was always looking outside the box, trying to find long-shot solutions that nobody else had thought of. For example, one week he said he was going to go to plumbing school and then apply to NASA to become an astronaut, because they'd surely need irrigation system technicians on Mars someday. A week later, he had a bulletproof scheme to get one percent of every FHA loan owned by dead people, based on a typo he found in some HUD documents he found at the library. None of these things worked, but he always poked holes at the edges of the reality dam, hoping to make it burst.

Me? I constantly had dreams of flipping into the other dimension, about somehow creating something that would blow minds or create another reality. And I toyed with it at times, but it never worked, and I kept trying anyway. Definition of insanity.

Anyway, here we are. Describing another trip that didn't work out, and ignoring the fact that it all started through some weird wormhole portal that I should probably monetize until the point when Tom Hanks is in the movie version, but I'm not exactly sure where the damn thing even is anymore.

* * *

I kept walking a giant loop through Ted Stevens International, looking at the various stuffed bears and moose and helicopters and bush planes hanging from the ceiling. I pretty much had the whole place to myself, just the strange high-latitude amber sunlight coming through the windows. I thought about how I could find my own distraction like Lars seemed to do every week, but I was honestly out of ideas. I just wanted to get through each week and then spend the weekends worrying about the next one.

Right before I went to stock up on twenty-dollar bottles of water and sit for two hours before my flight, I saw a familiar looking door next to the Chili's Express. It said 98036-0181 on it. Looks like I just saved myself a half-day of flying, I thought.

Evel Knievel Would Never Call Me at Five in the Morning to Talk About Christian Black Metal

Tornado outbreak, film at eleven. Ezra Pound was still alive and on a mad poetry rampage, straight out of the mental hospital for the criminally insane. Live-tweeting from his death cell in Italy, he's posting Slayer lyrics and launching a new breakfast cereal on Kickstarter. "Nobody can fully explore hate until they've competed with General Mills. Try my new Chocolate Cantos Crunch. Make it fast, your time of sorrow. On his trail, I'll make you follow!" The cereal would later cause extreme heart damage, anorectal cancer, fatal sepsis. God hates us all.

Storm chasers stocked up on diesel fuel and pub cheese, the cheapest form of protein and fat at the truck stop, totally keto. Carb-free is the new punk rock, said the reporter at the anti-everything rally. If rat poison had a multi-level marketing scheme with a high referral code rate, they'd be eating d-CON as the new miracle cure out in the square states. Die free or die. And why chase tornadoes when you can sleep in and look at the destroyed trailer parks later? It doesn't get you as hard, but there's less traffic. (Also, I know I shit on keto a lot. Sorry about that, do what makes you happy, I don't care. Just try not to make it so bacon is like three dollars a slice when I order a burger.)

The all-holistic rub-and-tug at the top of the Rocky Mountains offered rolfing with full release. Three for two with a GroupOn advance purchase. What they didn't tell you is you had to put high-octane gas in your car so it didn't ping and misfire above ten thousand feet. And every mile-high gas station used their own refineries, their own high-ethanol gas, their own formulation. Total taxation, five bucks a gallon when it was only a buck and a quarter down at sea level, and that E15 fuel will melt the rubber hoses in any old car. Communism, said the farmer who gets paid by the government to plant corn and burn his crops for no reason.

The massage "therapist" wouldn't shut up about the superfund sites and toxic pollution in town. He looked like Jim Croce if he ate an all-McDonald's diet for fifty years straight. "That biomass plant south of town is obstructing justice. I'd like to see that place burn to the ground, except we'd have to smell it. The straight-up odor of shit on any regular day. They had to close the Schlotzsky's Deli just downwind of there. Didn't even take out the equipment, just chained the doors shut, lit the sign on fire, and left town."

"Fuck Schlotzsky's," I said. "You can't have a New York deli from Austin. It's basically just Subway sandwiches for people who are too unhealthy to eat at Subway. And don't even get me started on their flatbread pizza bullshit. Tomato sauce and plastic cheese melted to a piece of cardboard. Whoever had that genius idea for their menu should be sent straight to Guantanamo for extrajudicial execution."

"They had to close that deli because it was built on the outpad of a chemical refinery that pumped straight kepone into the well water. Every cashier who worked there had a three-headed baby with telekinetic powers. You don't get birth defects like that from making sandwiches all day, even if you work at Arby's."

After the "massage" I felt like I needed to find some medical licensing agency and narc him out. He was out there operating without any decent restraint, totally beyond the pale of any acceptable human conduct. I wanted to be healthy and hike in the mountains like those spandex-clad REI couples I saw all over Denver, which was a stupid idea, but it involved buying a bunch of clothing and gear I'd obsess over and only use once, so I was totally onboard. Drove to a mountain lake caused by a nuclear weapons meltdown or UFO landing or some other industrial accident. Maybe it was just a reservoir from a dammed river, but you know how rumors start. Beautiful scene, pristine water, mountains in the background — looked like a life-size Coors beer can label. But I can barely stand at nine thousand feet, let alone hike five miles.

I drove back home, thought about nuking a Hungry-Man dinner, staying up all night writing some stupid book about a UFO cult. I jotted down the start of an arbitrary manifest I could never finish before giving up for the night. Even after chugging four of those energy bomb drinks, I fell asleep on the couch watching *Papillon*. (LOL at Dustin Hoffman shoving a pair of coke-bottle glasses up his ass.)

About the Author

In 1974, I wrote a patent for a new method of interstellar space travel based on the *Interplanetary Voyage* game for the Magnavox Odyssey. I got help with the typing from a high school math teacher with a methadone problem, and he tried to take credit for the entire thing. He later became obsessed with a theory that the Phish concept album *The Man Who Stepped into Yesterday* was about the Richard Nixon assassination. The teacher was shot by a Secret Service agent at Fairchild Air Force Base in Spokane, Washington, and died of sepsis a few months later. The patent was never approved.

Some of my first published work was a fake board game review column written for a friend's zine about scab fetishism, titled *Sanguineous Thrust*. I was fired after writing a review about a fictional pornographic *Warhammer 40,000* expansion set called *Whorehammer 40,000*. Games Workshop filed a cease and desist against the zine, and said they would sue the publisher unless I was fired. The publisher destroyed all issues in which any of my work appeared. He later became a fact-checker for *Elegant Bride* magazine, until Condé Nast ceased its publication in 2009.

In addition to fiction, I've written several true crime books on my theory that John Belushi was responsible for the Chicago Tylenol murders. I'm also a nonprofessional architect and was an amateur doctor, prior to being told by the State of California to stop practicing medicine.

After I did the layout for this thing, I had a mostly blank last page, and it was bugging me, so let me jot down some serious stuff I won't put in the Kindle version. This year has been impossible for all of us, and everyone I know has lost friends, family, and their general sanity, either figuratively or literally. You'd think being locked up all year would mean I could write a dozen new books, but the constant anxiety has been killing me. I wrote about 100,000 words of a sequel to *Atmospheres*, and it makes no sense releasing it. Self-publishing is dead, and a manic tale about the apocalypse is a tough sell when people can flip on the news and see a more absurd version constantly. I still write every day, but it's hard to make sense of it. That's what led to my short little outburst in the titular title of this book. Sorry for going meta with that.

I should thank the people who have kept me partially sane. Big thanks to John Sheppard, for the daily exchanges and keeping this failing publishing house going. Also thanks to Keith Buckley for joining the fold, and Jeff O'Brien for prooofing this stupid thing. Thank you for the Shame Eating crowd, even though Facebook is killing us all. And thanks to Ray Miller for the last thirty-five years of friendship. Lastly, thanks to you for buying this, especially the print version. No thanks to Evergreen Ford in Issaquah.

This is my seventeenth book. I still blog at <u>rumored.com</u>.

www.ingramcontent.com/pod-product-compliance
Lightning Source LLC
Chambersburg PA
CBHW061231170626
46809CB00007B/2627